DR. JUICE JORDAN: STANDARDS MATTER
Workbook Edition

BY EDDIE SMITH

ISBN 978-1-63944-571-4

PUBLISHER'S NOTE:

This work has been published and distributed in collaboration with

Maadist Publishing LLC. All rights and privileges are retained and

reserved by the original author and 14mediaproduction LLC

TABLE OF CONTENTS

I dedicate this book to those who adhere and fight for rules, order, and standards. Know that your influence and authority is greater than you may believe.

TRUTH

All truth passes through three stages. First, it is ridiculed. Second, it is violently opposed. Third, it is accepted as being self-evident.

--Arthur Schopenhauer

Author's Note

A leader is the principal member who commands a group or organization. A leader's responsibility is to encourage, support, and coach those in their organization. Being a leader requires more than simply telling people what to do and then expecting them to carry out their duties effectively. A true leader is both inspired and humbled by the designation.

Jackie Knight invites us to witness her journey in her leadership development. She learns that leadership is about service. This type of leader is confident and builds the confidence of the group. Effective leadership is more than having positional power over a group or having control of others. Dr. Juice Jordan shows Ms. Knight that being an effective leader is not determined by your physicality, age or gender. Leadership is about establishing standards and faithfully upholding them. When led with established standards, others will follow.

As the author, my experience encompasses over 30 years as an educator. This includes classroom instruction, administration, athletic director, and coach. As an athlete, I was fortunate to have been coached by great leaders. My professional experience and exposure to these greats led me to identify the common denominators of successful leadership. They are respect, responsiveness, accountability, inclusivity, and influence. This workbook edition is designed to develop leaders. To inspire them to believe and commit to their organization's mission. Standards really do matter.

What does effective leadership look like? Without standards there is no measure by which to analyze and evaluate. Without standards, how will you assess the action steps needed for growth and development?

"The quality of a leader is reflected in the standards they set for themselves."—Ray Kroc.

PREFACE

In the twenty-first century, many educators feel defeated at combating negative student behavior and apathetic academic performance. Permitted student misconduct with increased cumbersome regulations placed on teachers destroys the learning environment. However, there is a ray of sunshine in this darkness. He is a man who opposes this movement. Some label him an agent of change, a revolutionary. He is fearless when challenged by parents, teachers, or the School Board on issues that deny students their right to receive a quality education. His actions either make you an ally or adversary. His mission is to create better thinkers. He brings truth and action, and under his leadership his school thrives. He is well-trained, effective, and unstoppable. Some equate him to a superhero. His powers are not mystical, but they are real. He knows that a person without standards is like a balloon lost to the wishes of the wind.

1

*"You're right, Stryker. I lost my way. I lost my humanity. I forgot who I was…but then something happened – Something I didn't expect – **I was reborn!**"*- Luke Cage.

It is crazy how you can see something, and it triggers a thought filed deep in your memory vault. Before my first year as principal, teaching in the classroom was an intense rollercoaster ride of emotions that took me up, down, and around. It was the first day of school and there were many things to accomplish in so little time; yet I noticed a letter on my desk. I saw the name on the letter, Juice Jordan. Excitement filled me. Many of us allow only a few people in the special rooms of our heart and he was one of its tenants in mine. The first day of school is like the first time you meet a person. That meeting speaks volumes of what is to come. Seeing this letter awakened my curiosity. I needed to read at least the first line to quench my thirst before going to my duty post. The summers fool educators in to thinking they have plenty of time to get things done before the students return, but it is never enough time. I opened the letter and read the first sentence. The words blurred as I drifted in thought. I remembered clearly.

In a speech made by President Obama he communicated the following: *if we do not have parents who are constantly emphasizing high levels of achievement, if we do not…tell kids that their primary focus is to learn and that they are letting themselves down and…letting their country down when they do not succeed, we are not going to be able to compete.* I reminisced about the early years.

Superheroes in comic books and movies are mystical, yet I still love to watch them. I cherish the moments to see them exert their powers. Part of me wished I had a superpower. As quick as my fantasy moved in it faded to my reality. I did not care. It was my private moment to dream. I thought about the price a superhero must pay for their extraordinary ability. Some people love you for it and the "haters" conjure up a way to destroy you. Then I thought about the people dear to me. When a superhero's identity is revealed, life for them is never the same, nor the people close to them. What would I do if I had superhuman strength? I glanced at a colleague, "What would he do if he had it? Would he use it for the moral betterment of humanity or for selfish gain?" I looked at my watch. It was time to start the next period.

I have often heard it said that the paths we cross are not coincidental. What I did not know was that my journey would cross the path of a man who was considered a superhero. It is funny what life has in store for us. Like so many, my sheltered world shut me into my own selfish desire of what I wanted from life. That was what life was about, right? I played my part and acted as though I cared about being a part of the team, but my real focus was self. It was about strengthening my career and building my retirement. I understood the world's system. It promoted a dog-eat-dog mentality. I accepted that and knew I would do what I needed to advance. As a teacher I felt undervalued, and I wanted out of this classroom madness. I figured that an administration position was my ticket out. I confirmed an interview with a Dr. Juice Jordan for a vacant assistant principal's position.

There are a few times in a person's existence when he or she will experience a life-changing moment. The encounter is so powerful it can alter the course of a person's journey. Goals are a natural part of human life. Yet, some people are not very concerned with achieving them. To me, not having goals are synonymous with driving with no specific destination or intention, because there is no purpose.

My mom and dad were loving and supportive, but I thought their strict rules were too tough. Their expectations were high, and at times, their pushing me to succeed made them come across as slave drivers. You know how young people think when it comes to adults who constantly tell you what to do. Relentlessly, my parents instilled in me standards that would lead to a quality life. At times, their pushing me toward greatness made me feel like a machine, but they taught me to cultivate my emotions. Unlike some kids, I did not have the luxury of doing what I wanted when I wanted. I hated it then but now I am thankful for structure and discipline. How can anyone accomplish anything without the two?

I had been a teacher for seven years when my aspiration of becoming an administrator resulted. The constant classroom misbehavior of my students and the lack of parental support had done a number on me. Yes, I blamed the parents. My mom often reminded me that the young parents of today lack proper parenting skills. She was right and I saw it every day. Parents should prepare their child for how to act appropriately in social settings and respect the person in authority. I loved teaching, but each day became more of an emotional grind. I hoped that my seven years in the classroom would give me the credibility to be an administrator.

The end of the school year was close, and summer break was days away. I looked forward to it every day that I entered the building. I needed a long break to recuperate and get back my sanity. I had enough of the classroom. I took a moment to assess myself. Really, it was a moment to sell myself on the reason for wanting to leave. I was an African American woman who taught at a middle school where a chaotic environment was the norm. As a collective body, the teachers were not cohesive, and the administration was biased. The administrators chose which teachers they wanted to support when it came to addressing student misconduct. It was late in the school year and most of the positions at different schools were filled. I went online to our school district website to peruse available job openings. That was when I saw the assistant principal position. My negative ego screamed that I had no chance. My positive side knew that I could not give in. I focused on my breathing and positive thoughts to gain control. Fortunately, I was accepted for an interview. Getting the job was a long shot, but I figured I had everything to gain and nothing to lose.

I knew I needed to do something. I was sick and tired of being sick and tired. I knew my reasons for change were for selfish gain, but at that point I did not care. I recalled days when I literally heard screaming, running, and playing in the hallways during class instruction.

My students and I often heard a "phantom knock" at the classroom door with no one there when one of us opened it. I often questioned whether I worked at a school or a recreational facility. Even with my classroom door closed, the boisterous sound was disturbing. The shrill of the screams in the halls were a clamorous disruption. My students looked to me for help, but I could only shrug my shoulders in bewilderment. Most, I guess became desensitized to the disruptions, but I could not shake the ill-feeling it gave me. I worked hard at not becoming insensitive to this environment, but there were many days when hopelessness overwhelmed me. I was not able to teach, and I knew the students were not able to learn. My bleakness was watching them fall into a dark abyss of nothingness.

It was commonplace for my students to come to school one or even two hours late, several days out of the week. The parent's actions clearly communicated to me that getting their child to school on time was not a priority. Their attitude came across as though I should be grateful, they sent their child to school. Some of the students lacked proper nutrition and hygiene. Others wore the same clothes for two or three days straight. It was easy to detect the stains on their unwashed clothing. It was perplexing how they were not teased. Anyway, I never heard any negative comments regarding that issue. The funny thing was that some of my parents were at home when their child left for school in their neglected manner. How could any student concentrate on academics when deprived of necessities?

Many of my students were from low-income family households that needed government assistance. Mom and dad (if present) worked hard to maintain a sustainable income. But most of the parents mastered the art of "entitled assisted living." Some students did not know their dad. The idea that a student has not ever seen their biological dad was interesting to me. I thought about my parents and how I was raised. My parents never let making money overshadow their engagement in my activities. They aspired but understood their responsibilities with me. I have lived by that paradigm, and because of it, I was unwilling to accept mediocrity. I wanted the same for my students. I hated to see them settle for less with a poverty mindset. Achieving their best was what I wanted

4

for them.

In my early years of teaching, I assumed the parents of my students were my allies, but I was proven naïve. I learned that you cannot base what other people would do on how things were done in your household. I learned what is acceptable to me may be unknown to others. Leading a horse to water does not mean that you will make him drink. It was different for me. Mom and Dad were engaged in my education. They volunteered at the school, communicated with my teachers regularly, helped with my homework, and supported my extra-curricular activities. So, in my first year of teaching, I assumed that all parents did the same for their child. Not so. A few of the parents did, and I mean a few! I soon learned those parents who are supportive and those who are not through the first encounter or telephone call.

I learned quickly not to look for help from my unsupportive parents. Those parents were more difficult to deal with than my student having an "episode." I have experienced times when a mom would come to the school and interrupt class instruction to chastise their child. If my class was fortunate, it was spared the profane language; even though, I knew yelling and the distinct sound of leather was guaranteed. On those occasions, I had to intervene and remind the parent that physically disciplining their child on school campus was prohibited. Making the call to the parent was justified, but their form of resolution did not help.

That type of battle was an everyday affair, and the multiple years of stress had taken its toll. There were times when I questioned if I really wanted to work in education. Many of my days felt like being on a battlefield. I was tired of fighting classroom disruptions with student misconduct. It had become obvious that meaningful learning was not the focus. Even when I followed school protocol, it seemed like no serious consequence was administered to the student. I made it through seven years and now I knew I needed a change. This classroom war had ravaged my emotions. I was exhausted at policing students, and I needed a way out.

That way out was my reason for applying for the assistant principal's position. From my perspective, being a school administrator or an instructional coach was my path to sanity. I knew those positions

5

had their issues, but I felt they did not experience as many issues as I did as a classroom teacher. Plainly stated, teachers were at the bottom of the totem pole with the crap dumped on us. It was like in the movie *Staying Alive* when John Travolta talked about everybody dumping on everybody. His dad's boss dumped on his dad. Dad would come home and dump on his mom and mom would dump on the kids.

The assistant principal's position was at Washington Middle School under the leadership of Dr. Juice Jordan. Washington Middle was once known as a breeding ground for anarchy. The school was infamous for having juvenile delinquents. There always seems to be one school in the district that is labeled the worst. This school was recognized by the national public schools association for having the lowest standardized test scores in the southern region. How any teacher made it through a complete school year was amazing. I heard that it was a place where you feared for your safety. The district implemented changes through many principals, hoping that one of them could turn things around. The culture of the school was chaos and ruinous. Unfortunately, even though each principal signed a three-year contract, each only lasted one year. I felt like that was my environment. It was not on the same intensity level as Washington, but it had enough stress to make you not want to return.

After years of turmoil, the School Board announced that it had one option remaining. They turned over the leadership reins to Juice Jordan. He was their last option and if he could not lead the school in a positive direction, the doors would be closed, and the students rezoned to other area schools.

I received a call to interview for the assistant principal's position. It was scheduled for 9:00 am on Thursday. Wow, I was surprised! I did not want my thoughts to sabotage my hope. I thought about the qualities I could bring to the leadership table. My grade level chairperson experience would not be sufficient. Vacillation is a destructive struggle. I made myself thankful for being considered for the interview. My subconscious mind reminded me to choose the possible over the impossible.

Days passed bringing me closer to my interview. The fear of the unknown fiercely attacked what confidence I had. The angst of the wait was brutal. I knew the days of waiting were close but when you are ready for something to happen, one minute can seem grueling. I did my best to keep my mind calm and relaxed. I just wanted it to be over.

Ultimately, my big morning came. I made sure to arrive early to get my thoughts together. I entered and took a seat in the office. Mrs. Bond, the receptionist, was pleasant. She made me feel comfortable as I waited, which helped a lot. I am sure she could sense my nervousness. I turned my attention to how fortunate I was to get the chance to interview and that I would give it my best shot. I humored myself during my wait. It is quite funny to say the name of Dr. Juice Jordan. It made me think of a medical doctor who stressed the importance of good health! I scoped the school's decorum. The age of the building is apparent, but I can tell that it is well-maintained. The tile floor has a glossy shine, and I notice that if I look down at the right angle, I can see myself. The interior lighting is bright. There is an inviting softness in the building that made me feel welcome. Some school offices can give you the feeling of an insipid government office where the wall embellishments are lacking and uninviting. Maybe that is why the people who work there seem unenthusiastic. If you are not in good spirits, their negative disposition can overtake you. My nose caught a whiff of a pleasant fragrance of vanilla. Yes, it is quite inviting to be here.

I take advantage of my wait time by practicing my responses for the anticipated interview questions. This calms my anxiety. My parents raised me to be a thinker and an achiever. I became aware in my late teen years that my mission in life was to inspire people. My thoughts wandered. I got my mind back on track. Why did I think I was the right person for this position? I was sure he would ask that question. I prepared a simple answer, "I have a thirst to inspire students."

Influence drives a person. My mom is a brain surgeon and my dad a professor at the University of Atlanta at Georgia. You could easily deduce that they were people who had lofty goals and high expectations for me. Mom and Dad believed that opportunity is always available, and it is a person's responsibility to go after it. They taught me that life circumstances should never be an obstacle. I thought about the analogy of weather. Nature can produce climatic storms with varied levels of intensity. Some are strong enough to cause considerable property damage. The owner of the property is at the mercy of the storm. He must let the storm take its course, and afterwards, assess any damage. For the owner, this is the opportunity to move forward with needed repairs so that the home is hardy to withstand future storms. People must do the same. Circumstances should not be the reasons for quitting but for achieving. It is my commitment to be stronger than any storm. A strong dose of confidence shoots through me. My champion attitude reveals itself.

Belief is a necessary virtue of achievement. Belief coupled with action makes things possible. In the beginning, a person may not have a detailed plan, but it is belief with action that brings a solution. My students would share their dream, but I needed them to understand that it takes more than a dream to create. Dreaming is easy but a dream without action will not become reality, and I was committed to helping.

It is unfortunate when a person tolerates a stronghold of disbelief. It denies their creative power. It becomes a powerful, destructive tool. Daily, I recalibrated my mind to not accept the stigma of no hope from my students. My parents modeled for me what a successful life looks like. Thinking big is a prerequisite. Big thinkers cause cities and nations to be built. Without them, there would be no progress.

Sometimes to inspire these young minds, I learned to look at myself as an underdog. See in the competitive world, the underdog is often expected to lose. However, with strong belief the underdog can bring a mighty fight with victory. There is a difference in the effort of the boxer who fights to win, versus the one who fights to defend his title. The underdog has nothing to lose and leaves nothing on the table. However, the champion fights cautiously to not lose his title. The underdog's victory is a triumph that has an indescribable elation that runs deep. I received that intensified feeling when I saw my students light up with epiphany. I loved to see the underdog victorious, so I encouraged my students to think the same way.

My power comes from my mind. The world can lead you to believe that power is measured by one's stature. If you are tall, you are qualified to lead. If you are beautiful, you get more opportunities than those who are not. Truth be told, a person's physique does not automatically qualify a leader. Although, I must say that my 5'11" brown curvaceous frame is gorgeous. I will concede that beauty may get you noticed, but it takes a beautiful, scrupulous mind to qualify a leader. My beautiful mind makes my physical presence undeniably attractive and powerful. I glanced over at the window where I was sitting. I was at the perfect angle to see the full detail of how I looked. I took that moment to recheck my makeup. My shoulder length hair is natural. I was never one for hair extensions and I did not hate on women who prefer it, but natural is my way. I noticed my blonde highlights. My hair designer did a fantastic job! I looked down at my long, toned legs. Everything was in place. Hmm, these Jimmy Choo heels feel great. Dag, I must say that I looked marvelous! I am almost about to slap myself. My peripheral vision kicked in and I notice Mrs. Bond smiling while looking my way. Hey, what can I say? A girl must make sure that she is representing her best.

A few minutes passes when Mrs. Bond alerts me that Dr. Jordan was ready. I followed her to his office. With each step, I felt my heart pounding. The intensity of each beat feels like a subwoofer speaker. I wondered if she could hear it. We made it to his office and with a warm smile he thanked me for coming. I take in his appearance. He is well-groomed. As he shakes my hand I noticed his nails are manicured. He is wearing a White Egyptian Cotton Shirt with French cuffs. It embellishes his four-button grey Glen-plaid three-piece suit. My eye-tour takes me down to his black Salvatore Ferragamo shoes. A million thoughts seemed to run through my mind. Everything seemed to move in slow motion. I expected to see a man with an intimidating size, yet he was not. "Please come in and have a seat," he said. I admired his clean-shaven head. Bald is striking on the right pate. I clear my mind to refocus. Dr. Jordan commences with the history of the school. He informs me about the background of how the school was established and the uniqueness of its construction. His interview approach is not what I expected. I expected the traditional approach where I would talk about myself and what made me the right person for the job. Basically, the traditional process becomes a grandiloquent moment of bragging about what you have accomplished and hope that the interviewer takes the bait.

"Please call me Dr. J," he stated. I thought about Julius "Dr. J" Erving, a former NBA All-Star. I learned about him while hanging out with my dad and his love for professional basketball. My dad watched all his games. I loved being around my dad, so I watched the games with him. My dad taught me about the connections between life and sports. Jordan's approach was interesting I thought. He shared the school's mission and vision statement and his plan for meeting it.

Dr. J. questions my philosophy on education. It brought me out of my listening trance. By this time, I had become relaxed. My posture was comfortable, and my breathing was calm. I glanced at the clock. Time was moving quickly. Throughout the interview, Juice proposed hypothetical situations and asked how I would address them. I understood that he needed to know how I would react in each situation. I appreciated that process. It gave me a better perspective of what I knew, did not know and what I felt comfortable addressing. When we completed the interview, Jordan explained the follow-up process. I thanked him and went on my way. I was curious about what he thought about me. Anyway, I was glad it was over.

That night, before going to sleep, I processed the events of my day. I thought about the interview. I think I did a decent job, so if I did not get the position this experience would be accepted as beneficial. I consider it to be a steppingstone to the next level in my career. I was lucky to have the opportunity to meet a legend.

I noticed that the more I relaxed, the clearer my mind screen projected what took place in my day. Dr. Juice asked what accomplishment I was most proud of in life. I thought about my purpose for teaching. I responded, "Some of my most rewarding moments were in the classroom. For me life is about supporting and educating. I decided to use teaching as a vehicle by which I could make those virtues known. Many of my students come to school accustomed to a negative home environment. I wanted to be a catalyst for growth and impact in their lives and the community. What better vehicle is available to where I could add value in this world?" Juice asked, "Do you think you're an effective teacher?" His question made me think deeply. "At this juncture in my career I'm not one hundred percent sure. I can only give you my subjective answer." "Why?" he asked. "I have an answer, but it may not be a politically correct answer." I pondered more. I could have easily said through my positive interaction I am infecting my students with good, but that would have been a false statement. Sometimes people spout off saying what they think others want to hear. During my time with Dr. J., I knew he was not a man you could butter him up with a lie about education and think he would buy it. I answered truthfully. "Moments of doubt attack my mind." I look at Juice. What is his assessment of me? It was then that my dubious ego stepped forward. My sane personality fought hard to fight for control. Surely, Juice was familiar with my work experience before inviting me to this interview. He knew I was inexperienced at the administrative level. I tried to make myself feel good by justifying why I should get the position. My mind questions why did I accept this interview? It was becoming exhausting. I needed to end this back-and-forth doubting match. Talk about worry. I added to my response, "I like to think that I am a positive impact on them. Yes, I do think I am."

Dr. J. asked, "Do you believe you were able to help all of your students succeed in life?" "I would love to think that, but truth is that I don't think so," I answered. "Why?" he asked. I thought for a second. Did my answer come across as uncaring? I paused before answering, "I would be proud to say that I have save all, but human behavior shows that it is not possible. A person must want help. Children's behaviors are developed from the model they are exposed to at home. Because they eat, sleep, and play in that environment, they become rooted and grounded in it. Hopefully, their school environment offers a positive model to offset the one at home. Nevertheless, it's up to each person to make their choice." "You mentioned the word choice. What choice do children have?" asked Dr. Jordan. "They can make the decision to make right choices and live by standards for positive gains," I answered.

11

Juice continued, "Growing up, what was your viewpoint of life?" I must have raised my eyebrow what seemed like ten times before answering. My memory of age 11 put a smile on my face. "I had fun growing up. Eleven was around the age when I started to understand myself. I like to use the analogy of a stuffy nose. It is a great feeling to be able to clear my nasal passages to breathe clearly. Eleven was my age of clearing. I enjoyed school and my pastimes. My parents worked hard and had high expectations of me. I just figured that was how life was for all kids. They made me work but they were encouraging and supportive. Both attended my school conferences and school events. Any personal issues I experienced, they talked to me about them. I never gave it much thought. I mean, I figured that all parents did the same with their children. Mom and dad always asked me questions which I felt helped me to analyze and evaluate in life. Just the simple process of asking questions helped me to think about issues and consider the other person's perspective. I have to say that was one of the most valuable tools I gained. It taught me to consider other's feelings. It did not mean that I would always agree with that person, but it helped me to understand their humanity. I think those experiences matured me when it came to decision making. It also helped me to connect with my students. I learned that students will not work with you if they do not feel a connection with you. They need to trust that as a teacher, you bring a safe space for them to be. Also, my parents allowed me to earn my freedom through trust." "So, do you feel they provided structure?" he asked. "Unequivocally, I had structure and boundaries. The freedom I am talking about entailed being able to think freely and ask questions about issues. By doing so, I learned to analyze and evaluate matters. When I followed through on my responsibilities, I earned their trust which gave me opportunities to prove my independence. I learned to flourish within my boundaries. They instilled in me that right thinking causes right actions which are necessary to change the things you do not want. Having a negative attitude never produces favorable results."

"Do you have any hobbies?" asked Jordan. "I love to read books on "how to " and inspirational stories of other people's lives. Their story inspires me. We all have our issues, and it is interesting to learn how they overcome them. *The key to a successful life is not preventing problems, but how to respond to them.* People in general get so worked up and deny what I call their "organic nature." It is in our organic nature where we relax during a circumstance which allows our subconscious mind to present us with the solution. It is in our thinking whether we win or lose. I love to read about their journey to their solution, but I have learned an important caveat. In my problems, I don't look for my answer through another's experience." "What did you mean by your last comment?" asked Dr. J. "Looking at someone else's solution to be my solution could cause me to overlook my solution which could lengthen the process." Juice paused. His finger and thumb were pressed against his temple in a pensive position.

Dr. J. closed out the interview with, "The world is moving at a fast pace and if things do not slow down, something drastic can happen. Your life is worthy of finding your mission and pursuing it with every ounce of energy. Once you find it, there is synergy between you and the vision. Anything outside of your mission is wasted time that cheats society by not giving a worthwhile return. True living is more than working for an income and a pension. Most have settled for going to a job, but not me. I have work to do. My gifts and talents are designed for my work. When I edify the people, and the people edify me. Great leaders who live by standards know that a great leader is not all about having all the answers."

I awakened to the annoying sound of my alarm. My eyes slowly adjusted to the sunlight. Morning comes too fast. We are at the end of the school year, and I feel uninspired to return to the classroom. My interview stirred a fire within me. I had a strong desire to do more. I made a pact with myself that no obstacle would slow me down from getting promoted. Truth had revealed to me that promotion no longer was about running from something but to something.

A week passed when I saw I received a voicemail from Washington Middle. Simultaneously, I was doubtful and hopeful of the news. I had that moment when you wanted to know but you didn't want to know. I listened to the message with crossed fingers. I heard the excitement in Mrs. Bond's voice. Dr. Jordan offered me the position. I had ten days to sign the contract. I wasted no time to return her call. I labored to contain my excitement. The volume of my voice was high. I'm sure that I was yelling but Mrs. Bond was kind to let me continue. She instructed me to go to the district office to human resources and sign my contract and any other necessary paperwork. A smile was plastered on my face. Each time I passed a window, I could see all thirty-two of my pearly whites. This feeling reminded me of the holidays. After some time of letting this great feeling soak in, slowly I collected my composure and called my mom to share the good news.

Mom was equally ecstatic. I believed the volume of her voice was louder than mine. "Jackie, you know your dad and I have always believed in you. You do know that, right? Baby, how do you feel? I can see you impacting more students on a larger scale. I am so excited for you, and I know your dad will be also! We love you." My mom asked questions, but obviously, they were rhetorical since she never allowed me to respond.

My remaining days were joyous. My promotion lifted the weight of my present environment. I focused on my departure. I was in a blissful state even though the stormy environment around me swirled. It was like standing in the eye of the storm. Although the chaotic storm winds whip around, the eye is safe. I called Mrs. Bond to see if Dr. J. needed me to take off a few days to move my things there. She informed me that he was busy and would leave him a message to return my call. I went about my daily duties.

Juice returned my call. I was perplexed with his answer concerning my intentions on an early move. I anticipated that he would tell me to move in immediately, but he advised me to wait. He was not in favor of me taking time off from my current position to set up things in my new position. After listening to his explanation, it made sense. "Finish strong where you are before transferring," he told me. "Your current principal will respect you for it. Besides, you never know when you may need something from this person and leaving now without closing properly may offend him. Offended souls can be unpleasantly disagreeable when you need something from them. This is one area most people take for granted. Believe me, I understand. The person leaving is only concerned with his desire for departing. However, some are oblivious and unconcerned with where they currently are. They tend to get sloppy and unprofessional in their current position which sends a message that they do not have respect for their present organization. And for spite, your principal could impede your transition." Juice made his point. I took his words to heart.

Committedly, I finished the school year strong. I felt at ease knowing that my transition was soon. It was amazing how often I began to reflect throughout the day on my classroom experiences. Some things I did came by error. I am thankful those mistakes did not come back to bite me in the butt.

At my school the staff's teamwork sucked, the work environment was counterproductive, and selfishness ruled. The blame is contributed to the principal. Anarchy was our norm, and it was the principal who permitted it. I have studied successful organizations and their leadership. Those leaders placed priority on relationships and ethics with their staff. The employees in those organizations stated they felt valued, which inspired them to perform at high levels. Lord knows that we needed to know that we were valued. As a teacher, I worked on my relationships with my students. I wanted them to feel valued. One way I did so was to converse with them about matters. It matters to people to be able to express their opinions. Of course, there were boundaries with how and when. There are times when it isn't appropriate to ask why or to express your opinion. I think it behooves leaders to understand how the people in the group think and feel concerning issues, processes, and progress. Great ideas can come through sharing. A dictator does not last long, and micromanagers can choke the life out of the group. History has proven that. Under a dictator's regime, the committed employees leave and the rest plot how to overthrow the tyrant. The more interest I showed in my students, the better they performed. Well, some did. My answer to the question of how to change things is logical. Change the thinking at the top, and the thinking below changes.

Here at Carter Middle, we were divided into cliques. The staff who were the so called "in good" group sided with the principal. Those who considered the "outsiders" learned to be silent about issues so as not to be a target. I made my circle of association small. The less people the better chance of not having a spy among you. Some teachers did speak out on issues in our meetings, but they soon learned that the administration did not want their opinion. Administration claimed they respected our opinions, but their words were empty. When a teacher openly expressed a repercussion followed. It did not take the teachers long to realize the truth. The funny thing was that the issue the teacher raised was valid. I wondered if the same was happening in other schools. To conclude, those who were wise never let their gripes travel far from their lips.

I sympathize with the new teachers. Their excitement is great. However, they are naive to the demands and stress that comes with teaching. Before earning their degree, I wonder if they were informed about the bureaucracy of placing a student in the next grade when he did not earn it. What about a student who earns a discipline referral for his misbehavior for the fourth offense and not receiving an appropriate consequence? To a teacher, it can send a message that discipline, and order are not priorities. What's wrong with that, you may ask? Think about how this action impacts those students who are doing what is asked of them with behavior and academics to see those students not being held accountable are allowed to continue. All students know who didn't put in the work to qualify them being promoted, yet they are. Those scenarios are only a taste of what happens. Each school presents different challenges. Personally, I felt a sense of unjustified pressure from my principal. She knew how to covertly add more duties on my plate without unethically crossing the line. I wasn't a numbskull. I had to walk gingerly while keeping my head down. I think back to what Juice said. He was correct about departing on good terms. Now was not the time to cause spite.

There needs to be more support systems for teachers. We need an emotional and physical outlet to maintain a high-performance level. I did not know exactly what that should look like, but I knew something needed to be in place. The expectation of teacher responsibilities swallows one. A rubber band is made to stretch but there is a limit before it snaps. It was debilitating working in a chaotic environment. Our good teachers had a short shelf life at Carter. Good teachers are like gardeners. A gardener knows for thriving plants to grow it first needs cultivated soil. During the growing stage, the garden may produce weeds, but over time those weeds must be replaced with more "good seed" to maximize the garden's beauty. Our administration didn't practice the application of standards for a fruitful garden. Their philosophy consisted of shifting blame on the teachers for student underperformance. The supportive parents spoke up for a changed environment. They wanted order for their children's increased academic performance. However, their effort was to no avail. Their plea fell upon deaf ears, and I felt their frustration. How must it have felt for them to follow protocol to see no resolution. In the end, those parents withdrew their child. Carter Middle School was like the La Brea Tar Pits in Los Angeles, California. Once an object fell into the pit, it was trapped and lost. Were we developing global leaders or dependents? Welp, why cry over spilled milk, right?

A huge smile formed as a surge of energy flowed. Dr. J. selected me—Jackie Knight—to be on his team. I felt proud of my accomplishment. My time here at Carter was complete. My farewells would be few. Only a couple had a special place in my heart.

At the end of each workday, I transitioned my things to my new office. The office walls were bland. They did not agree with my decorum. Some artwork and a beautiful rug sufficed. I was thankful my office was spacious. Dr. J. walked in as I was in deep thought of what more I could add to embellish the office. He welcomed me as I unpacked. "Ms. Knight, you will learn a lot here with an open mind. I am sure you will catch our passion quickly. I will be your support system. Do not be stressed about getting everything right. Keep in mind the school's mission. It guides everything we do here. Never compromise. If you do, you compromise us as a team, and a compromised team weakens and divides; a team divided always fall and I will not permit that to happen." He paused, "Are you ready?" "Yes, I am," I replied. "Trust that I have your best interest at heart when it comes to your leadership development. I know the type of environment

17

you're leaving, but that is in the past." Hearing those words for the first time from an administrator felt liberating. The way you make a person feel is a powerful tool. I had not experienced leadership like his. I was nervous, but even in my nervousness I told myself that I was ready. Each time I repeated that affirmation to self my confidence rose.

Something to think about:

When you are talking, you are only covering what you already know. The only way to learn what the other person needs is to ask questions—over, under, and all around the topic conversation and then listen to the answer. —-The 7 Powers of Questions, Dorothy Leeds

What is your takeaway from this chapter?

Do you think you are where you want to be in your organization? If not, what are you willing to change to get there?

_____

_____

_____

_____

_____

_____

_____

_____

_____

_____

_____

_____

_____

_____

_____

_____

_____

_____

_____

2

"Because some men are not looking for anything logical, like money. They cannot be bought, bullied, reasoned, or negotiated with. Some men just want to watch the world burn." - The Dark Knight.

Juice shared with me his love for education and would always consider himself a teacher. "Ms. Knight, may I share my reason for becoming a teacher?" Educating the youth excited me. I appreciated how he shared information about himself. His sharing gave me the idea on how I can carry out my duties. I recall in my first year as a teacher, I noticed unhappiness on the faces of the veterans. I did not give it too much thought. I just figured it was from their length of years in the profession and their return to work from their summer vacation. What became apparent was the impact of the environment. As the days passed, the negativity grew. I knew I could not be my best under those circumstances. It was inevitable that my solution was to transfer. I've heard it said that doing the same thing over and over hoping things will change is insanity. There was no need to stay there thinking that things would change. Going to work there was like driving to a cesspool plant. If I did not leave soon, my positive thinking would be corrupted. Please know that I did not consider myself superior, but I was smart enough to understand this damaged environment. When in Rome, do as the Romans was not a motto I cared to adopt. I had high goals to achieve." The conviction in his voice was strong I thought."

Dr. J. continued, "Learn wisdom through credible people. Mr. Othello March, a former colleague, gave me wisdom to apply in my first year of teaching. He said that the typical teachers say they are teachers of a content. Unlike a typical teacher, he knew he was a teacher of students. In that moment, it made sense to me. I had never thought of it like that. I was not teaching a discipline but students. Othello made his statement and quickly walked away. His statement felt like a hit-and-run incident. I had never considered that fact but after hearing his comment, it became apparent. From that point forward I adopted his philosophy. When someone asked me what I taught, guess how I responded? Try this experiment. Ask five teachers what they each teach and listen to their response."

"I read something that defined education as anything that increased awareness," stated Dr. J. My mind turned to my mission in education. I sensed a connection between what Juice told me and my experiences with my students. I did want my students to become better thinkers to be productive in society. Othello's wisdom was on the mark. Many people offer their advice about things. Sometimes they don't bother to ask if you would like their wisdom. You cannot accept every person's advice. There is a caveat. People may mean well, but everyone is not qualified to speak into your life.

Is there a connection between March's statement and student disinterest? Is the lack of interest in our students due to the lack of enthusiasm of the teachers? Energy is shared among people whether it is negative or positive. My mind started to peel back the layers and delve deeper into thought. What about tradition? Is it synonymous for keeping things the same? Is educational tradition a killer of enthusiasm in learning? How do students grow and develop without consumption of effort?

Juice continued, "I became an administrator to reach more students on a larger scale. I believe a person can learn at any age whether he is a student or teacher. Human beings are amazingly adaptable creatures. The core of learning is in the person's self-image. How a person views himself determines what he will achieve. His failures and successes are determined by his self-image. Put my statement to the test. Think about what I said and your low performing students. Is there a correlation between the two? As instructors, we believe our students can do more, but a negative self-image impedes their belief from greater achievement. These students cannot perform above their image. Truth is that a person's thoughts form their attitudes, feelings, perspectives,

23

and beliefs. The sad thing is that some do not take the time to reflect on their own thoughts.

At that moment it registered to me why some parents who had bad experiences at school perpetuate that cycle through their child. This parent, as a student, may have had a teacher whom he or she did not like. The reason for not liking them varies. This trauma for the parent can perpetuate through their child and teachers. This type of parent often displays obstinate behavior for an unsupportive relationship with their child's teacher. The school becomes a target of blame. For students to be successful it takes parents and teachers working together on a united front. Kids are smart. It doesn't take them long to learn the line of expectation. When they see disharmony between their authority figures, they will cross those lines.

My thoughts surfaced in my beautiful mind. I now see that wanting to become an administrator was for my own selfish gain. I wanted to rid myself of the headaches of the classroom. Having shared this time with Juice, I can see how life is blurry with unfulfillment if you're not contributing a positive change in your community. Now with a changed perspective my vision is new and filled with hope.

Dr. J. finished with, "We can talk more during our campus rounds. Go ahead and handle your business." As he leaves my office, I could hear him say, "The world is a classroom." I continue unpacking my items. Embellishing my space is a desire I love. My eyes scan the room. Where to place my plants, pillows, and candles? My mind went to organizing my files but that can wait for tomorrow. I set out my rugs next to my desk. My body clock tells me that it is time to end this day. A fresh start is never a bad idea.

The next day, Juice and I made our campus round. I loved having this time. It gave me the opportunity to glean knowledge. I grabbed my notepad for our walk and talk. It's prudent to write down information rather than trying to remember. Juice reiterated information on the history of the school. He shared his perspective of the parents and student body. The barometer of community involvement was a talking point. He stated, "When I first accepted this job, our anarchic school was a handful for the administration and the teachers. The students loitered in the halls during class transitions. They didn't show any concern for going to class after the class bell. Many of the students were infamous for their indecorum toward the teachers, custodial staff, and the administration. There was no shame in using profanity in the hallway, classroom, media center, cafeteria…well you get the picture, don't you?" "Yes, I do. This made me think about the environment of where I left. In an environment of such, the students can't learn, and the teachers can't teach."

"You're correct. The ironic thing is that the students did not like coming here," Juice laughed. "The school board offered me this prospect. Its poor reputation was well known throughout the district. I could sense the School Board's uncertainty of me turning this school around. However, I had faith. I knew with the Board's support that it would be a matter of time for my confidence to generate success."

I recalled my experience at Carter Middle. I had the worst feeling about having to go to a place that at best tolerated you instead of celebrating you. There are many who go to a job where they are disenchanted with their leadership and their work environment. He continued, "I didn't sit before the Board with grandiose promises or a 20-point action plan. I kept things simple. One thing I did stipulate in my contract was a 3-year guarantee. I knew that it would take that amount of time to accurately show gains. They inserted a clause agreement that stated if I could produce signs of academic improvement each year, the 3-year agreement would be honored. Personally, I knew we would turn the ship around 180 degrees within the first year. A major part of this plan depended on the full support from the Board. There would be major pushback from uncooperative parents once the culture shifted."

"Are there any major lessons learned to share once you were in?" I asked. "Yes. For the record, let me set my foundation that upholds all that I do. There are standards that I apply and to hold myself accountable. Without standards, people do what they want. Without standards there is inconsistency throughout the organization. How do you hold a person accountable if they don't know them? I made a commitment to myself that as the principal, I lived by the school's mission statement and stuck to the policies that were in place. I guess you could say that I was relentless like a Jack Russell Terrier. I decided there are three kinds of people in the world: allies, adversaries, and neutrals. The interesting thing about the neutrals is that they will eventually pick a side when presented with a strongly felt issue. Issues always revealed their true belief. Never compromise your beliefs, and do not get too comfortable with your allies. Even with that, do not walk around leery of everyone. It is a waste of creative energy, thinking that all people cannot be trusted. Just like you, every person has a personal agenda." My eyes were trained in on him. I received his energy. Juice leaned in and quietly said, "Trust yourself, your judgment, and look within to find your balance."

I found myself feeling like a student. I was amazed at how I hung onto his every word. I had a sensation of wanting more of this shared wisdom. If a student does not make a connection with the concept, learning can be delayed. I had a connection. This was more than passive information. Juice had a way about him that challenged my way of thinking. I began to question traditional methodologies and processes in education. *Why are things done the way they are? Does the school legislature really want to remedy the condition of low performing schools? What is really the mindset of the school boards regarding student policies? Are policies accommodated for the elite students at high performing schools and everyone else suffers the change? Is it possible that poor performing schools are permitted by design?* My dad once told me that broken programs bring in additional allocable funds. Each year, more teacher accountability is imposed with less from the students. I dialed myself back in to focus. Juice's leadership encouraged me to be at peace with work. There was a calm feeling in my surroundings like receiving the aroma of vanilla potpourri. Effective leaders invest in their people. Dr. Juice was investing in me. I had this feeling that I could not clearly express in words how important that was to me. Here, I felt valued.

Dr. J. continued, "I sent out the school's vision to the parents, teachers, and the businesses. I wanted all parties to be aware of our mission and to join us as stakeholders. If all parties weren't committed, we wouldn't be able to change things in the area. My approach was to make it difficult for these kids to lose." I got it. To make the change successful, he made all entities take ownership. A culture where blame takes the forefront cultivates an environment of chaos. Tolerating poor performance from one person could set off a chain of another and then another. This would prevent the achievement of the vision.

"Jackie, I don't believe threats are effective in disciplining students or the teachers. Simply, I act on the policy in place. Kids and adults decide their actions in life. Over the years, I've encountered few in authority who held those under their leadership fairly. When that leader did not issue appropriate consequences for their misconduct proved unwise. It felt wrong to hear adults repeatedly give directives to a student to stop their misbehavior. The teachers would give idol threats toward the students with the intent for them to follow directives. Humans are smart. A person observes what a person will or will not tolerate by your actions, not words." "What changes did you see in your staff?" I asked. "Yes, my staff. I evaluate my staff's production carefully before making recommendations of keeping him or her on board. I did not base my decision solely on mine or another's observation. I like multiple people assessment. This helps me to be sure that I'm making a wise decision when it comes to making a recommendation. What I do can impact a person's life significantly. Providing a quality education is priority."

Before I knew it, we had covered the entire campus. Juice suggested handling priority items before going home but not to stay late. On my way-out Mrs. Bond's path crossed mine at Juice's door. We could see him sitting in a pensive position. She tells me, "That is his typical position. He is an intellectualist who constantly encourages people to think. Our behavior is based on our self-image." We smile and depart.

Our pre-planning days were different than what I was used to at Carter Middle School. I expected to see apathetic looks on each of the teacher's faces. At CMS, the teachers did not want to return, even after having their two-month summer break. But our teachers seemed genuinely happy to be back. I consistently saw smiles. This was new for me. Everyone was cordial with greeting one another. This was an indelible moment. As the days passed, I saw that Dr. J. was a man of his word. I could see that he respected other's time and by his actions proved it. Juice said he believed time was best spent on productive things. Minor issues could be communicated through email. Professionals know how to read and act accordingly. Why meet about something when you can read for yourself? He didn't believe in meeting unless it was something that needed to be discussed by the group.

Dr. J. started our first meeting with the school's mission statement and a quote, "Misplaced purpose inevitably brings destruction. While you are on this team, always keep the school's mission in your forethoughts. The mission is your purpose for being here. Any other reasons are misdirected. Failing to focus on this will inevitably decrease student achievement. The school's mission is so important that it is the center of all our discussions whether in faculty meetings, parent-teacher conferences, or PTA meetings. Our decisions are based on it. Teachers, direct your students and parents to the Student Code of Conduct manual. If we encounter a parent who has a different agenda that counters the school's mission, we respectfully remind him or her of our mission. I understand some parents advocate for the benefit of their child only. I believe he or she does not mean any harm, but our educational model is not a Burger King's model. They cannot *have it their way*. Encourage them to be receptive to the fact that there are multiple ways to reach a destination and to trust that we have all our students' best interests in mind. Encourage them to keep sight of the goal and believe that it will be reached. Teachers, please align your actions with our school policies. For example, when I am addressing a student's academia or conduct, I base my actions on the school's handbook. If I deviate from it, I make myself vulnerable to an emotional decision that may be a wrong one. I'm not willing to gamble and neither should you."

The planning schedule showed that the veteran teachers could opt out of meetings designed for new teachers. Juice left it to the teachers to be accountable for their needs. If you weren't able make it to the original meeting, there was a make-up training session held before or after school. Whichever the option, your attendance was noted. I loved how the planning schedule was printed out for the staff. This allowed a teacher the flexibility to set their calendar. Juice believed that professionals should be afforded the opportunity to manage their business. The teacher environment at Carter Middle was administration led which meant the teachers had zero input. We felt powerless in the meetings. I always thought the teachers should be involved with most areas of the profession. However, they weren't. I'm sure most teachers would love to speak about how they aren't treated as professionals. They could openly share their thoughts about it. I am certain they would tell you that most meetings were redundant and superfluous. I recall countless times sitting in meetings that I felt were not beneficial. My time would have been better spent working in my classroom or lesson planning. Micromanagement kills the spirit of teachers. The principal at CMS micromanaged her staff. I hated being under that type of leadership. It stifled my creativity. The more control she craved, the more she crippled our school. Why was it so hard for her to understand that fact? Professionals know their responsibility. When leaders treat adults like children, they will rebel against their system. The same goes for our students. I saw teachers who attempted to control student behavior. It was a taxing situation for them, and it consumed too much energy trying. Time was better spent teaching students how to be autonomous. When students understand their role and are freely allowed to operate, they will meet the expectation.

After the formal welcome to the teachers and staff they were free to attend to their business. Some went to their respective meetings and others decided to work in their classroom. As the teachers filed out of the cafeteria, I heard one of them ask another teacher for help with something in her classroom. The person asked gladly responded with an energetic yes! Her response shocked me. I was not accustomed to hearing others helping. I was feeling good about this place. But how will it be when the students return? I would some have my answer.

On the first day of school the atmosphere was still as the students entered quietly. I greeted my parents pleasantly as they entered. They knew the procedure for visitors. No reminder was needed to go to the main office to sign in. There was a line of parents to sign up as volunteers. For me this was a new thing to see. Our business partners stopped in. Some of our vendors donated water, notebook paper, and snacks.

One of the business leaders from the Chamber of Commerce asked me, "Ms. Knight, welcome to our family. How are you?" "Great!" I responded. "My name is Galore Love. Did you know you were working with a great principal and a great staff? I have seen many principals come and go. But none of them compares to Juice and what he has done. We love him as a leader but even more as a person. With honor our community donates as many supplies needed. It is a small trade for what Dr. J. is doing with our students. We know they are well educated and job-ready when they graduate. We have waited so long for this result and now that we have it, we refuse to let go. Again, welcome and enjoy." "Thank you and I know will," I replied.

Dr. J. posted himself in the façade to greet the students and parents. Some students came over to greet him with hugs. Afterward, they went to either the cafeteria for breakfast or to their homeroom. Our morning transition went smoothly. I decided to move about to interact with the teachers. In passing, some teachers told me brief stories of what the school climate was like before Juice's arrival. The hall transitions were a chaotic nightmare. The students would loiter. The teachers constantly yelled at the students to get them to move. Some teachers would not say a word to get students to class. Plainly put, "The students ran the school." I made the connection to that story. That kind of environment reminded me of the toxic energy of a youth detention center. It was then that I gave thanks to the universe.

The events of the day flowed smoothly. Contrastingly, the teachers here were on point with their duties than where I left. Dr. J. came by to ask how my day went. I mentioned that things went well and that I love this environment. Juice shared some wisdom. "I selected you as our assistant principal because you are the right person, and I see you having a bright future. I will provide a comfortable space for you to acclimate. Gain from your experiences. Always remember that you're a champion."

I heard his words vividly, but the fullness of his communication would take time. I was truly excited about education. I was excited about working with kids. I felt rejuvenated. My best response to Juice was, "Absolutely." I could see that Dr. J. was a man of great wisdom. He spoke with anecdotal points. His actions were with purpose, not haphazardly. Ah yes—purpose—is what determines our day. I remember what Juice said in a meeting about purpose. Human beings are goal-driven creatures. People who understand this are wise. They are visionaries who get things done. I wanted to be a member of this society.

Juice continued, "I want you to lead our parent conferences, staff meetings, and business meetings. This will be plenty of interaction to help you get your feet wet." As he shared, I could feel my eyes widen. Did I look like a deer paralyzed by a car's headlights? "You will be fine," Juice stated. I will be at each meeting to support you. Before the meeting, you and I will prepare with background information regarding the issue. Remember to keep your focus on the school's mission. Regardless of the present emotion, stay firm. During the first couple of meetings, I will model for you on how I lead. Typically, I will start with the meeting's purpose and our agenda. We use this reference to keep all parties on point. After each meeting, I replay it in my head for the positives and negatives. That is my way of working on my game for the next meeting. I want you and I to reflect and share our thoughts. How does this sound to you?" "It sounds good to me," I replied.

I take a moment to think about the impact of Juice. He is amazing. I it was crazy, but I could see why some think of Jordan as a superhero. His leadership influence is inspirational. This is what is needed to encourage those to become a strong administrator. My parents were right. There are few people who will cross your path with enough influence to transform your life. These people are called change agents. Juice Jordan metaphorically has thrown me a life preserver in my ocean of peril.

Looking ahead…the year progresses, Juice has kept me on pace. I lead the faculty meetings and the community meetings. He and I talk over important information before going into our meetings. At Carter

Middle this didn't happen. There was no briefing before entering a parent conference involving a delicate issue. Going into those meetings, I always felt that I had to defend myself. It was a feeling of being on an island by myself. My administrator would sit in the meeting offering no words of support. Now, I see what support looks like.

A friend of mine who owns a fine dining establishment once told me that the quality of their dishes wasn't determined by the talent of his employees, but it is the chef following his system. The consistency of the dish was the application of the system. Talent of staff is key, but an effective system is greater. It prevents inconsistency of the desired result. I have read where the top Fortune 500 corporation leaders know that successful leadership starts with having the right people. Having the right people who understand the need for plugging into a proven system, and the right people are internally inspired to achieve their successful results. The right people are driven by internal goals, not external motivation which is short-lived. Yes, the right people know that without the right system an organization is doomed for failure.

Some companies believe that hiring experienced people is the key to organizational success. I read an article that broke down a perspective on the concept of successful hiring. The criteria for hiring experienced candidates are a hit-or-miss approach. Traditional expectation is for the candidate to be experienced in the position. But this approach is not one hundred percent perfect. Consider the scenario of an inexperienced mechanic versus the experienced mechanic. Which is the better hire? Most would choose the experienced mechanic. Their thinking may be that the experienced candidate would bring the knowledge and wisdom needed to the job. Less money and time wouldn't have to be consumed to train him. However, the contrary perspective of the inexperienced candidate is that he may show a greater propensity to follow the organizational systems. The inexperienced mechanic is apt to follow his trained steps to complete the task. The experienced mechanic is inclined to do things his way. Complacency and overconfidence are a hindrance to the job. He is more apt to take short cuts in the jobs. His overconfident nature makes him prone for glossing over the details by doing things his way. It is interesting how being a veteran at something can be a detriment or a benefit. I reflect. I think my theory is on point.

Returning to reality, our school systems are in place. All I needed to do was to plug in. There was no reason for me to create a new way of doing things. That was good for me especially since this is my first year in this position. Juice has been at this school for five years. The teachers and staff are now what I call operating on autopilot. The student standardized test scores have risen each year. His teachers teach with inspiration, not motivation. Motivation is what he considers to be a temporary external stimulus. Dr. J. believes that it is the person's responsibility to inspire. Inspiration is a quality that powers from within.

As the year progressed, things came together to make sense. Juice is a master at getting people to analyze and evaluate their thinking. It did not matter your age or your title. His purpose in life was to infect people with a purpose for improved thinking.

In one of our conversations Juice shared this moment. "A person's self-talk is core. I was told that a person talking to himself means that is not right in the head. My perspective has changed. What you say to yourself has the power to build or destroy. Our accomplishments are based on what we believe, and those levels of belief increase when our self-image increases. How we see ourselves determines what we do in life. When a person envisions that they deserve something in life, their self-image rises to the same level of expectation. Our self-talk powers and drives us to achieve that belief.

Parents are pivotal when it comes to the shaping of their children. What they say and how they act model expected behavior to their child. Their words are powerful. They can build up or destroy their child's esteem. There is a fine line that can easily be crossed if not careful. Let's consider a student's mediocre performance in a class produces a below expectation of the parent. The parent cares, right? He lovingly tells his child to try harder, to study harder. Most would agree that this encouragement is a typical response from a parent, right? It sounds logical, but the cure may not be in studying more, or studying harder. A better resolution is aimed at inspecting the way the child views his work and showing how changing the way he thinks can attain better results. How defeating it can be to a child that is really giving his or her best effort to be told to try harder or study more? Disenchanting this is. I can see how some students developed low self-esteem. It doesn't take much effort for the student's "mental monster" to create fear, worry, and doubt."

"Juice, I hear you saying that a parent should focus on changing how their child's mental image." "Yes. A parent needs to teach their child how to appropriately question his or her beliefs. To teach them that a person's performance is a direct result of how they perceive self. Eventually, deficient thoughts shape a child's identity. For example, a failed performance on a test can tell a student that he missed his target (passing grade). However, defeated thinking tells a child that he or she is a failure. That kind of thinking is dangerous. You see that student has attached failing to themselves to be a failure. Do you know the general concept of how a missile works? A missile has a guidance mechanism that re-corrects itself to hit the intended target. Once it is launched, depending on the distance of the target, a missile can veer off. There are outside influences that can impact the object. The missile has an auto correct mechanism within that will bring it back on course until the target is hit. Can you see where I am leading you? A person is like a missile with a goal as his target. He launches himself to go after his target. After his launch, outside influences create distractions and if strong enough, those distractions can cause him to veer off course of the intended causing him to not reach the target. Eventually, he may develop negative thoughts which form negative attitudes and emotions. He brands himself a failure. He is easily identified by his comments of "I can't do anything right" or "I'm not smart enough." Going back to the parent and how he or she thinks is crucial. Wrong behavior from wrong thinking can be passed on to their child. A parent's paradigm is effortlessly passed on to their child and the cycle continues."

I understand the importance of Dr. J. investing in the staff's modality of thinking. He recognized that the result of one's duty is related to the way he or she thinks. Skill application is important, but a person's way of thinking is the foundation for success. Dr. J. with his words painted me a picture of how it happens in an organization.

Continuing, "Wrong thinking impedes the mental and emotional growth of a person. During our PTA—Parent Teachers Association meetings, the PTA Board offer leadership development workshops for our parents. I know it may sound a little odd, but over fifty percent of our parent populace is young. Our data clerk compiles our data and from the results we know that fifty percent of our parent populace gave birth by the age of eighteen. We have a small percentage of parents that had a child by the age of sixteen. Albeit, they are parents, we cannot take for granted that they have effective parenting skills. Therefore, we offer our workshops. Hence, our PTA Board focus is on our parents' thinking before they discuss order of business. It works for us." I wondered if other leaders thought this creatively.

I learned more in my first year here than the previous seven. Credit to Dr. J's leadership. His encouragement of me to evaluate my results helped me to see what worked and what did not. My first school year as an administrator was enjoyable but it quickly came to an end. Having come from an unsupportive environment, it felt like heaven here. Dr. J. never let up on the idea of improving me. In return, I slowly got it. I accepted my duty to assist the staff as to become an impenetrable force. Together we were invincible.

I think about the last three weeks of school of my first year. Juice had summoned me to his office before the students' arrival. He asked, "Ms. Knight, do you recall us having a conversation where I told you that you were the right person for this position?" "Yes, I remember," I said. "This information I am about to share will give you a clearer picture of what I meant. This is my last year at this school. I am moving on, and I have yet to tell the staff. I did not want them to be distracted with my leaving. I know that if I had announced my leaving, the faculty and staff would be distracted from exercising their best." I got what he meant. An outsider may have considered his comment arrogant, but I knew that he was correct. Knowing what I saw here, the students, parents, and staff loved Juice. He was more than a principal; he was their superhero.

Juice continued, "At the end of the month, I'm transferring to Bethune Middle School. The Board has granted me an early transfer so that I can acclimate the new staff. This climate of this school is in a bad way and needs much work to get it turned around." As he talked, I had a moment of thought where I entertain walking away. I became a little salty about the news. I tuned back in to hear him say, "I will be in and out of the building finalizing things here. I need your assistance here with handling matters. Can you help me with this?"

I just got on board and Juice is leaving. I had mixed emotions swirling within. I was happy for him, but sad that he was leaving me. What would things be like without his presence? Dr. J. turned to walk away. Three steps later he turned back, "Ms. Knight you never asked me who will be the new captain of this ship." Hesitantly I asked, "Who?" "I don't know," he responded. Is Dr. J. playing? "I do not think the school board has finalized their decision. They've had plenty of time to locate a new candidate." So, the school board knew, I thought. My selfish nature reared its head. I love it here under his leadership. "Dawg!" Questions flooded my mind. Will the new principal work at developing the staff? How will this new leader inspire us? Will the new person value the current system or change things? What kind of personality will he have? Anyway, I needed to get off that ride. This change was not about me. My reason involves me committing to the school's mission. I will continue to do what is needed for the betterment of our students.

"By the way, you and Mrs. Bond are coming with me." "Wait, I stood there flabbergasted. Did you just say that I'm coming with you? Dr. J., I see that you got jokes." My smile grew. Dr. J. smiled as he walked away. Before receiving the good news, all I could picture is what our new environment would be like without Juice Jordan. There was part of me wondering if our school could maintain our successful culture.

It was on my way home that day that some of the details Juice shared sunk in. I was so thankful for Juice taking me with him. Being with him provided me with a great opportunity but I felt there was much more to experience in this business. Did I just say the word business? Truth be told, education is a business where major money is made. The real question is who makes that money? Well, I know it is not the teachers.

This first year as an administrator ended on a good note. Dr. Juice eventually made his official announcement to the staff that he was transferring to Bethune Middle School. Of course, as he expected they were shocked, happy, and sad that he was leaving. The staff wished him farewell. Juice made sure to tell them that that he arranged a contractual agreement with the School Board for them to honor their current system in place at WMS for minimally one school year after his departure. Typically, things aren't done that way, especially when a new person takes over as principal. I was not sure how he convinced the Board to go along with that, but they did. Then again, he is Dr. J. It would take a confident principal to accept those terms and not implement his own program. Juice continued, "I contracted that agreement for this staff because they are special. Besides, most professionals know there is a major adjustment period with a new leader. The staff needs time to acclimate to his style. If you are wondering how I arranged this, know that everything is negotiable. As with anything, having a proven track record encourages the process. Based on my performance the School Board agreed to accommodate my wishes. This was one way to help the staff emotionally get over the hurdle of my leaving."

Juice invited me to sit in on the last faculty meeting at the new school. He used that opportunity to introduce me to our new school and staff. The meeting was brief. He opened with the school's mission statement before welcoming all returning next year. I recalled his words, "He made the statement of understanding if anyone opted to transfer. Every person has a responsibility to self when it comes to their career. It will be a new year and new beginnings for those who stay. Please take note of those around you. Some will not be here at the start of the year. Some will be released from their contractual obligation during the school year. Accept this statement not as a threat but truth. I do not lead by intimidation. I simply uphold our school and district policies. Some of you have selfish motives. Selfishness is intolerable for our intended level of performance at BMS. Others of you have put in the work but have not seen the fruits of your labor benefit these students, this school, or the community. Our focus is teamwork. There are no islands here regardless of who you are or which department you work in. If we are a divided organization, we will not be able to satisfy our students, parents, or community. Negative attitudes will weed you out of this organization quickly. Regardless of your status, Ms. Knight and I will do what we can to assist you to your next destination. Know that Bethune's mission is to produce thinkers and doers for global advancement. Thank you and have a great summer!"

Juice's message was precise. As the staff exited, I heard murmuring comments, "Who does he think he is? Every principal that has come has said something similar and left us here with no change. These parents will tear this man to shreds." I thought to myself that this staff is in store for a reckoning. Actually, their comments fired me up. Yes, I wanted Juice to drive away the self-righteous individuals. Soon, they will know what it feels like to give up their personal agenda for the good of the group. Since working with Juice, my work has been rewarding and with the right people I was confident that we could empower our team.

Can you objectively summarize the chapter?

Is there a character in this chapter to which you can relate?

How does he or she impact your personal experience?

_____

_____

_____

_____

_____

_____

_____

_____

_____

_____

_____

_____

_____

_____

_____

_____

3

May Parker—*I believe there is a hero in all of us, that keeps us honest, gives us strength, makes us noble, and finally allows us to die with pride; even though sometimes we must be steady, and give up the thing we want the most. Even our dreams.* --Spiderman 2.

During the summer, Juice and I met daily to strategize our plan of action. Time seemed to escape my grasp. Soon, the teachers would return, which meant the villains included, who were sure to bring their negative attitude. I considerate their negative attitude to a high hurdle. If you are not in shape, you're not able to clear it. Even though our staff had veteran teachers, everyone would be new to Juice. Even the experienced did not know the kind of ride they were about to take.

Dr. J. had the welcome letter for the teachers mailed. It contained their assigned content, team assignment, and classroom location. My duties comprised of building supervision and the student dean for last names beginning with the letters A-M. The remaining students with last the last names with N-Z would be assigned to the administrative assistants. There are other models when it comes to this, but Juice thought it would be great experience for me to work with all three grade levels. I felt I was ready to handle it. Juice shared his wisdom that my discipline load would be heavy at first, but not to allow it to overwhelm me. He felt the intensity of it would decrease within a couple of months. As the building supervisor, if any teacher had an issue with pests, he or she would inform me. If there was an issue with their air conditioning system, I was the person to notify. Juice did not retain people that didn't know how to solve problems; he was not about babysitting adults. There were plenty of issues to address and he needed the right people in his organization to handle those issues. Of course, solving problems did not mean circumventing him. When it came to major issues it behooved the person addressing the issue to inform Dr. J. first before acting. It was better to be safe than to ask for forgiveness.

In this industry, educators needed an open mind to creative solutions. Being traditional was detrimental. Beware of the person that says this is how we have always done things. They are not open to new ideas and growth. Keeping things the same way equates to stagnation. Growth takes place when a person accepts challenge and acts on that challenge, even when it is uncomfortable. Growth means being stretched, but with a limit. There is a possibility of being stretched too far, to the point of snapping like a rubber band. Champions understand this.

Dr. J. structured our pre-planning schedule as he did at Washington Middle. He started the teacher's first day back with a general staff introduction and a brief agenda overview for the week. The environment seemed pleasant for the moment. Some had peculiar looks on their faces after they saw the schedule for the week. My conclusion was that they had never experienced being treated as professionals. I heard a teacher condescendingly ask another, "Is he just going to give us our schedule and release us to carry out our obligations like adults?" They would soon learn that working under this leadership meant not experiencing anything like their principals of the past.

Dr. Juice reviewed the game plan for the first week of school. "Teachers, handle your responsibilities. Be timely at your duty post. Do not feel the need to yell at students to get them to go to class or do class work. Learn to be at ease. Let your nature be pleasant. Think about how you would expect to be treated if you were in their position. The more you continue with the same actions you have been doing, the more you enforce your students to continue with those unwanted behaviors. Let your students be accountable for their actions. The importance here is that it all starts with you being visible throughout the school. Your visibility encourages safety for those students who are doing the right things. They need to see those in authority active. Take the opportunity to speak to the students as they pass. They are human beings. You are not the police or a prison guard." I saw a few smiles. Some sat in bewilderment. "Students will walk to and from lunch unsupervised. We will post personnel throughout as to encourage our students in the beginning to transition to their intended destination. There is open cafeteria seating. Yes, they can sit where they choose. Once they take their seat, they will not be allowed to move. A student can easily lose this privilege through loud or obnoxious behavior. He may have one opportunity to correct the inappropriate behavior, but any further occurrence causes him to be reseated or removed from the cafeteria. He will be reseated at an isolated table and if that does not encourage him, he may eat in a classroom by himself. Do not worry, we will have personnel sitting in the classroom with the student. Until our students grasp the Bethune Way, we will have regular hall sweeps for tardy students. Each time a student is collected in a hall sweep it will be logged and after the third tardy he or she will receive a consequence. Please be apprised of the students' code of conduct book. Over time you will notice some measurable improvements. Our key to success is how consistent we are with implementing the appropriate consequence, whether positive or negative. Are there any questions?"

No one raised their hand, but I could hear the negative sighs, masked whispers, and see their negative body postures. Were the teachers fearful about asking questions? Someone whispered, "Does he understand the type of student body we have here?" Others muttered, "Whatever he's smoking I want some. That plan is a recipe for a disaster." Juice finished with, "I ask that you document your observations of the uncooperative students. Formulate a list via email to your administrator regarding the student and any specifics about them. Your documentation is effective. Bear in mind, we will not consume an exorbitant amount of time for students who choose not to conform. Eventually they will make a choice to transform their thinking or accept an environment at a different location. By the end of the week, submit your list." Dr. J. ended with encouragement for the staff to get their rest and be ready for the next day.

After the meeting, Juice and I met briefly to summarize before ending our day. "Tomorrow, I want you to shadow me. You will be my extra set of eyes and ears. When opportunities arise, I encourage you to take charge. "Are you okay with that?" Juice asked. "Yes, I'm good with that," I responded.

The first morning arrived too soon. My sleep last night was off and on. I did not sweat it. My excitement was strong for this first day. I knew I could make up for it tonight. I took advantage of the opportunity of being up early. I made sure to prepare my clothing and to calibrate my mind with positive affirmations. I decided to wear my powerful Navy colored suit. I ate a breakfast of oatmeal and eggs and packed my lunch with a Philly cheese sandwich. I left early for work. I needed to arrive before the teachers. This is my duty.

I made my way to the front of the building. Parents presented themselves with various concerns as they filled the office. I overheard one telling how they have recently moved to the area and needed to enroll their child. Others were withdrawing their children. I was perplexed as to why they would be withdrawing, especially on the first day of school. Mrs. Bond must have interpreted my confused look. When I was close enough, she quietly whispered that some parents had unsuccessfully attempted to enroll their child into another school. Now they were forced to return and readmitted in BMS. The parent reason was an unforeseen technicality that stopped their transfer process. Whatever their reason, the office was filled. The air felt thick with tension. Impatience and disgust were the makeup on their faces. One parent had on her housecoat. Couldn't she have gotten dressed. There was one face that stood out. Her eyes were a deep red with a fixed scowl on her face. She stated her opinion strongly on how stupid this was that she could not enroll her child without proof of affidavit. Policies do not change to meet their needs. Juice caught me staring. "You see these parents knew the process before coming. This is not their first time doing this when it comes to school. They've adapted this chaotic culture, but it will soon change," he said. However, this was my first time seeing this. As a teacher, I was always in the classroom, away from this. These parents here are a far cry different from the supportive parents at WMS.

I looked at my watch. Right on time as I made my way to the doors to see the first students enter. Juice joins me. The first wave entered with an acceptable volume. We called it level 1. Level 1 is where only the person in close range should hear your conversation. Juice gave them a thumbs up gesture. He motioned for them to look at the sign above that read, welcome and quiet as they enter. The signage pertained to all that entered, regardless of their age. The students look up at the sign and put their finger to their lips. You know kids; it is their job to mock the adults. I could tell that the students were checking out us both. We were new to them. Students can give you a certain look of disapproval if they do not respect you. Their eyes cut up and down as they studied us with a slight twisted look on their face. I looked directly in their eyes to give an approval that I see you checking me and I am checking you.

At that moment, four male students entered loudly. I could sense negativity in their demeanor. Their action communicated that they did not respect this decorum. Dr. J. motioned for the boys to come to him. They acted as though they did not see him. I supposed they wanted to check Juice's poise. The second-time Juice verbally tells the boys to come. As they walked slowly to him, they continued to talk loudly. One in the group started with the "I didn't do anything" excuse. Dr. J. did not react. He gave a directive for the boys to go and stand alongside the wall until he called for them. They did. Students continued to enter the building. I heard a few say, "Already? School just started." Others shrugged their shoulders and shook their heads as they passed. The boys stood there for about 15 minutes. Wondering, why wouldn't he have them wait in the office?

Ultimately, the boys were sent to the office to be seated until Juice called for them. The office had cleared as most of the parents completed their business and went on their way. The last of the students have filed their way into the cafeteria for breakfast. Dr. Juice was firm on students having a healthy breakfast. He considered breakfast to be the most important meal of the day. Overnight, a person's body consumes energy and burns calories. A student that has not eaten a healthy dinner the night before and eats a poor breakfast starts his or her day at a nutritional deficit. For the remainder of the day, the student's body is trying to make up for that loss. Most adults know that kids, if not supervised, are notorious for eating unhealthy food. Students have no problem eating chips and cookies for breakfast. A body cannot perform at its maximum on such low-grade fuel. Low nutritional fuel means poor mental concentration. Not eating causes a person to focus more on hunger, not learning. Generally, the result is low performance, and low student performance frustrates a teacher.

Dr. J. allocated adequate budget for our school nutrition program. Some principals are so focused on budget cuts that they cut money in that area and their students suffer because of it. As Juice says, "What good is it to our school with money invested in text resources and computers and students aren't even able to maximize these resources due to a deficient diet?" Most administrators avoid this issue and act like it is not a recognizable fact, but it is. In Juice's opinion, schools were using money in the wrong areas. Until leaders wake up and see that the mental and emotional health of the student is priority before learning can take place, they will continue to get the same poor results.

The students finished their breakfast and headed to homeroom. I made my rounds in the café to speak to those remaining. I reminded a few to push in their chair and dispose of their tray. The food must be palatable as most cleared their plate. Each student was given a small bottle of water to take with them. Their brain needs the hydration for proper function. The empties were placed in the plastic recycle bin. Arrangements were made with a recycling company who would give back a nominal profit to the school. It was the school's way of going green. The money would be deposited into the PTA's account for future use. I liked that idea. It is an ingenious collaboration between school and community.

Dr. J. summoned me to his office to witness the boys receive their consequence. Each entered slowly into his office and took a seat. Dr. J. commenced, "Bethune has a new culture. All students who enter this school agree to abide by our policies, including hall transitions in a quiet, orderly manner. Everyone is expected to respect the processes of the school and in return it respects you." I glanced at the blank look on their faces with mouths ajar. Dr. J. continued, "Do you understand why you were asked to stand along the wall?" Only one of the four responded, "Yes." "Why?" Juice asked. The student answered slowly, "We entered the building in a loud inappropriate manner." The other boys sat speechless. "I appreciate your acknowledgement of my question. You are dismissed to your homeroom. Correct your behavior and do what is expected. You remaining students are going home for the day."

The look on their faces was priceless. They were surprised. Juice had gotten their attention. He looked up each student's home telephone number in the school's database. Of course, I could only hear his part of the conversation. He introduced himself to the parent and proceeded with the nature of his call. He told the parent that her son committed an infraction. Based on his comments, I guessed at the parent's response. "I understand," Juice retorted, "However, our culture here at Bethune Middle does not support this behavior. So, for today, I ask that you come to the school and pick up your son. He may return tomorrow and give it another try. He will be placed in the school's discipline cycle. This means that he will..." By his pause in mid-sentence, the parent must have interrupted with a remark. Juice continued, "If he continues to follow this path his record will become detrimental. Please have him picked up in the front office within the next hour. If not, we will have him escorted home by our student resource officer." Jordan hung up the phone and made his next call.

One of the boys asked, "Why am I being sent home?" Juice answered, "You will appropriately acknowledge adults the first time you're asked or told to do anything." The boy responded, "The principal last year only lectured us and then let us go. What we did was nothing. This suck." Dr. Juice courteously reminded them that Bethune's school culture is now different. The new culture meant that all adults would hold our students accountable for their behavior. We finished our business with the boys and moved on with our campus rounds. Each had

46

a sad look on their faces as they walked out of Juice's office. It was that kind of look a teacher loves to see when a student takes ownership and consequence for his conduct.

Anybody in education understands that the first day of school presents many challenges. Of course, there is a plan of action but with any plan, there is the unforeseen. Flexibility is a cherished virtue. The homeroom teachers were given extended time to thoroughly cover the expectations of our new culture. I wanted to get a sense of what was in the students' mind, so I sat in one of the homerooms. After hearing how the students would transition, one student in amazement responded, "I don't believe it. We are allowed to transition to our classes and the cafeteria on our own. I cannot believe it. We won't have to walk in a line like we're in elementary." The teacher continued, "Of course, loitering and tardiness has a consequence. Transitional times are not meant for hanging out. Hall sweeps are active, and it starts today. Students that are tardy are issued a tardy slip. The forms are duplicate pages. The top page is for the student and the second page is for the teacher. Your parent is required to sign the form and send it back to school. An automated telephone call will contact your house to inform your parent or guardian of your tardy or absent. Any student who does not have their tardy form signed and returned to their homeroom teacher will be issued an after-school detention. If you are a "no show" to detention, you will receive one day out of school suspension for each day missed. When given OSS, a parent meeting is required to admit you back in school. The meeting is designed for the parents and child to create a plan of action for improvement."

"Regarding a student who chooses to disrupt the learning environment, on the first offense, will receive a verbal warning to correct their behavior. Repeated offenses will be documented and followed with a parent conference. Teachers will inform their grade level principal when a parent does not attend the scheduled conference. A student will not be permitted to return to school until his or her parent shows for the conference." I sure did love the perplexity on their faces. "Each infraction occurred is logged under a teacher's classroom issues. Some of our students and parents are under the impression that your discipline record has no major impact on you, whether here or at a different school. Please keep this sage wisdom in mind. Any documentation, negative or positive, can be used for or against your benefit. Take time to read over your student handbook. It contains pertinent information. Bear in mind, not knowing our rules does not excuse you from breaking a rule. Ignorance of the law is no excuse for breaking it, even for the adults. An excellent focus for avoiding unwanted issues is to place focus on the school's mission." The teacher asked if there were any questions, suggestions, or complaints. For the students that raised their hand, they were told to write it and submit it in the suggestion box located near the classroom door.

I heard some students in the hallway. It was time for them to transition to their 1st period class. Since having sat in a homeroom period, I saw that it was a great move to extend that time, at least for the first day. As Juice said, "Time is the most precious resource in life and must not be squandered away." His philosophy was that every minute not effectively utilized is a minute wasted. Five minutes of unused class instruction seems trivial but multiply those five minutes over five days which equates to 25 minutes of lost instructional time for the week. Multiply that by 20 school days in a calendar month and look at how much instructional time is truly lost. Small increments may seem insignificant but big things start small.

There was so much to do in what seemed like so little time. Time seemed to move faster than ever. The end of the school day came in a "blink of an eye." I wanted to send out an email to the teachers closing out the work week on a strong note. I made sure to acknowledge the positives for the week on the grade levels. Information is powerful so I prepared the staff with agenda items for the upcoming faculty meeting. I requested the teachers to bring their list of difficult students who consistently disrupt classroom instruction or refuse to follow school policy.

The end of the work week came fast. I love my weekends. They are short, which means they are enjoyable. Typically, Saturdays are for handling personal business that you cannot during the week. Sundays are lounge days which always go too fast. By the time Sunday evening comes, I get that small, dreaded feeling that Monday is here, but now, I felt different since my role has moved from teaching to administration. I carried this excitement like a kid looking forward to going to an amusement park.

The next week rolled around quickly. It was time for our faculty meeting. As the teachers made their way into the media center, it was funny to me to watch them. Their behavior is like the students. You have some that are quiet and others that are loud. When they attend a meeting, most seemed to seat themselves at the back tables first, leaving the tables up front vacant; and yes, the talkers. The obnoxious talk while the

48

speaker presents. That was uncanny to me because teachers often complained how the students were disrespectful by interrupting their class instruction with their loquacious behavior. Yet, they exhibited the same behavior as the students.

Dr. J. adhered to the agenda. If there were any issues of concern that weren't on the agenda, he would table it for next week's meeting. I understood why. It was easy to get distracted and wander off the focused path. The goal of this assembly was to focus on students with repeated behavior issues.

One of the teachers asked for the definition of misconduct. Juice responded, "Misconduct is defined as an action that goes against school policy. These are the kids who display their choice to be rebellious toward adult authority. Their immoral thoughts produce substandard results, and at this level, our students have attended school long enough to know acceptable behavior. When a student chooses to disrupt a learning environment or resist a teacher directive, we must assume that they do not care to be here. Yes, I do understand their background may be influential and dictate a person's behavior. But that can only happen if that person chooses to let their past form their future. The parent is the model and influence for their child's world. Our role is to offer a learning environment free of unnecessary disruption. A truth not often stated is that we can only help those who want help. Our first PTA meeting will be held later this week, and in that meeting we will remind the parents of our school's mission." He asked the teachers to submit their current list of problem students to me. The administration will hold a Town Hall meeting during each grade level Connections. He closed the meeting and exited. He always had elsewhere to be. I recall his words, "We live and die by the calendar."

The next school day we held the Town Hall meetings in the gymnasium. Dr. Juice and I collaborated prior, "So Ms. Knight, how are things?" "Things are wonderful!" I responded enthusiastically, "For the most part, I feel comfortable with my duties. However, there were a few times when I felt overwhelmed," I stated. "Being overwhelmed is okay," he said. "Okay." "Yes, it is okay. You see growth occurs when you are stretched. You know the uneasy feeling that accompanies it. I know people do not like to hear what I am saying, but there is no growth when not stretched. I know it doesn't feel good, but a person must resolve to move forward with a positive attitude. It is all about progress, not perfection. Keep planning and work your plan. Planning alleviates worry. It keeps you focused and active at achieving vision. Planning blocks your mind from distractions."

"I see," I retorted. He continued, "A person is in either a state of becoming or stagnation. To reach a goal, a person must keep that goal fresh in their mind as they act. Champions know to evaluate their progress and score self. Without a measurable standard, how would they rate their progress of reaching the desired goal?" Dr. J.'s wisdom is an eye opener. "Ms. Knight, in the beginning, to build a vision it may not seem easy. As a matter of fact, it is not about being easy, busy, or difficult. People work hard at trying to do their role. Often people obstruct creativity by trying too hard. The key is to relax and let your subconscious mind supply you with the answers for achievement. Hence, a person becomes a being in their vision. Think about when people use the words "I am?" Think about those words. They signify that you are the thing of your "I am." Plug into your system and your system will supply you with your intended results. Be flexible and adaptable along the way. If you're not reaching your goal, it may mean that a different path is needed to reach your goal. Bear in mind that in this meeting we are going to discuss our expectations as a school and culture with these students. Be ready. I will lead."

We carried out our normal morning duties for the students' arrival. They entered quieter than they had the first week of school. All students were directed to the café for breakfast. Afterwards, they were released to homeroom. The teachers welcomed the students as they entered. Homeroom was an opportunity for the teachers to divert any student issues before they grew into greater issues. It was a time to set the tone for the day. Great teachers use that opportunity to build rapport with their students through encouragement, guidance, and discipline.

Students with low self-esteem typically have faulty thinking. Faulty thinking equates limitations, and possibly a deficiency in identity which is built on their self-image. A person will not rise above how they see them self. If their self-esteem is low, they tend to see themselves as a failure. This type of person tends to see everything in their environment as negative. That is why adults should consider the type of environment they produce for children.

Children need to hear that they are unique and talented. They need to know that they possess the ability to accomplish what their heart desires. Parents who do not tell their child these things are setting them up for mediocrity or failure. Children's mind is like a sponge that soaks up the stimuli in their environment, whether positive or negative, and without effort, feed their subconscious mind which produces their belief. If the child believes in a negative outcome, then his subconscious mind will work to produce it. A parent who tells their child he is not bright, he will soon believe that he himself is not bright. Eventually, he may feel unworthy and unable to accomplish much in life. Contrarily, how wonderful would it be if all parents would teach their child to have the right thinking? My thoughts flashed back to my parents providing me a healthy breakfast. Although our time was brief at the breakfast table, my parents asked me what was happening in my world. I loved that time because I felt important that they wanted to listen to me. I looked at the students as they entered. We have major work to do here. Maybe my thoughts were magnanimous. The foundation starts with educating students to eat nutritious foods and proper hydration. The major importance is teaching kids to have appropriate thinking.

Trust is major when it comes to building rapport with students. Teachers who connect with their students are more effective with instruction and having that connection equates to an open door. That open door symbolizes the opportunity to fill a vessel. It is a phase where value is established. Trust is a powerful virtue, but if it is broken, a teacher may not get a second chance to gain it back. Great teachers are effective at sharing their background to their students. Transparency strengthens that connection and shows your students that you are human.

During my daily walk, I saw a noticeable improvement in our hallway decorum. Student loitering had decreased tremendously. The students stopped and talked to their friends but moved on without having to be constantly told by the teachers. I noticed that many of the teachers have stopped yelling at the students. Of course, when working with people, you will have those that are resistant to change. The noise level was at a respectable level. The teachers were posted at their classroom door and greeted the students as they entered. Now, that was a cultural reversal in a short time span. However, there were still a few who decided to not heed the doctor's orders. The antagonists I called them.

Later in the afternoon, I gave the announcement over the intercom of the names of the students who were to attend this assembly. These were identified by the teachers as the arduous ones of misconduct. After the announcement, I made my way to the gym entrance. Slowly, the students made their way to the gym. Such perfunctory facial gestures most had. I guess I may have had the same expression if I were one of them. Was truth becoming reality to some? Juice started after the students settled in on the bleachers. I counted the numbers present. There were approximately one hundred fifty students. I recalled Juice keeping the meeting short and to the point. Why waste your time and theirs with talk? He requested the students to look at one another. As they looked, he told them to say their goodbyes. Melodramatically, some said goodbye to each other with gestures of laughter and fake crying. "For the record, you are passengers on a train departing from here. I am unsure of where your destination will be, but because of your current behavior, you have stated that you do not care to be a student here at Bethune MS. Where you go is a conversation you will have with your parent." Some quieted after his statement.

I lacked empathy for them. They consciously made their decision to rebel. I think it became a game for them to act clueless and irresponsible, but now their actions have become habitual. My thought shifted to my early years. Did I act the same when I was their age? Juice continued, "Because you each have refused to change your thinking and adapt to our culture, you will be moving on. Your teachers will not spend additional time trying to persuade you to comply with our school policies and meeting teacher expectations. We have students who value their teachers and their education. Those students have made the decision to do the productive thing. Their education opportunity will not be disrupted any longer. This meeting is adjourned. You may return to class."

This meeting led us to the next phase. I thought about the parents of those students who were in that meeting. How will they react? Would they give the excuse that administration targeted their child? Or will they file a grievance against Dr. J? Rest assured, a demand for termination would be expected. I looked at Juice Jordan posture. He was poised.

The arrival of the first Parent Teacher Association meeting was today. It was interesting to guess who would show, allies or adversaries? Time would tell. I sensed excitement in the air, like a major athletic game. I looked at my watch. Tonight's PTA meeting was scheduled to commence at 6:30 PM in the gymnasium. I expected about two hundred people. I communicated with the custodians to set out about 220 chairs and be ready with a go-ahead order to let out the bleachers if necessary. Dr. J. will be seated at the table facing the parents.

6:00 P.M arrived and memorable it was. I finished my last agenda item for the day. There was a last-minute detail for the PTA meeting. Parents sluggishly, yet steadily entered the gymnasium. I was surprised at how early they arrived. They entered in droves to where the planned seating was not enough. I asked the custodian to let out the bleachers. I did not expect that large of a crowd. Observing their faces, I could sense tenseness. A person's facial gestures let you know if they care to be there or not. The women were masterful with the cutting of the eyes. The men simply had that "I'm tired" look on their face, so do not bother me. Metaphorically, the denseness of the tension was thick enough to cut with a knife. I glanced at Juice. He seemed nonchalant about the affair. My mind raced with "what if" thoughts. Finally, it was time to start. Jordan opened with a few housekeeping reminders and followed with the mission of the school. He made some remarks in response to some parent complaints that led the Joe Clark story in the movie *Lean on Me*. I saw where he was going with this.

Juice prefaced with, "Joe Clark was asked to go into a school, as principal, to turn it around from a failing institution to a school where kids could learn. His mission was to give his students hope and aspiration. Here is a movie clip from the movie." The lights went off and the scene played. Mr. Clark was meeting with the parents regarding the behavioral students. Some students had been expelled for failure to comply with school policies, maintaining passing academic grades, or not going to class.

The scene begins…*A supportive school board member opened an emergency meeting with the parents of the expelled students. They were irate and demanded the meeting. The Board Member tells the parents that after a long hard day, Mr. Clark agreed to meet with them. A parent, Ms. Barrett, stands up and takes lead for the other parents on the matter of their children's' expulsion. She tells why her son, and the other children need to be back in school and not on the streets. Ms. Barrett goes on to share that the children who were kicked out of school are smart but have been discouraged with the chances they have in the community. Now that they were kicked out of school, what kind of jobs or hope will they have to work for? There is a war out there and these kids need all the help they can get.*

The parents in the audience were emotionally charged. Ms. Barrett was playing on their emotions, getting them in an uproar. You can hear some of the parents yelling for her to sit down, while some were yelling in support of her outrage. She did a fantastic job at instigating. The school board member cuts in to give Mr. Clark an opportunity to respond to her statements.

Joe Clark responded, *"They say one bad apple spoils the bunch, but…what about three hundred? Rotten to the core! Now, you are right Ms. Barrett. This is a war. It is a war, to save 2700 other students. Most of who do not have the basic skills to pass the state high school exam. Now if you want to help us, fine. Sit down with your kid and make him study at night. Go and take your names off welfare. Give our children some pride. Let them get their priorities straight. (He pauses) Dr. Mayfield, the school board president, offered me the opportunity to come to this school. After the offer, I fell on my knees asking God, "Why have You forsaken me?" And the Lord answered that I was no damn good if I did not take this job. God instructed me that I needed this job and do what needed to be done, and He did not mean that I was to be polite. I needed to do whatever to transform this school into a special place. A place where the hearts and souls, and the minds of the young can rise! Where they can grow tall and blossom. Out from under the shadows of the past, where the minds of the young are set free. And I gave my word to God, and that is why… I threw those bastards out! And that is all I am going to say. Clark got up and walked out…*

The parents were riled up. Some were yelling and aggressively pointing their finger at Juice. I thought they would leave their seat to get after him. Five minutes of time whittled away before the crowd quieted. Juice continued, "This movie is a representation of our situation and your rebellious kids. Please understand that Bethune Middle will not enable this misconduct. As a school, we will hold our students to a high standard, and we need for parents to do the same. Your child's behavior is their responsibility and yours. Our school culture does not promote disrespect for authority or our rules. The kids who come through these doors must decide to do the right thing. They want to improve their thinking abilities and are willing to who work hard academically and aspire to become great. They have accepted to not be cheated anymore in this learning environment."

"We want our students to feel good about coming to school. They will not be intimidated any longer by rotten kids. Our community is waiting for Bethune to do its part by mentoring champions. The life of our community seeks effective, qualified students. If you have any complaints, you may direct them to the district office."

Juice got up and walked out. The parents were in an uproar. I could hear words like, "Who the hell is he to tell me how to raise my child?" The PTA president speaks on the microphone. She attempts to get control of the crowd. It was futile at that point. In a brief break of noise, she was able to inform the parents that their agenda items were tabled until the next meeting. Juice's action sparked inspiration within me. He dedicated his life to bringing positive change and authority to the youth. He did not vacillate on when to give appropriate consequences. Standards mattered and were the criterion that permitted freedom and creativity for the students to perform. Juice made it clear to everyone that the youth were his mission. His commitment was unbreakable. I know it sounded crazy but the song by M.C. Hammer— *Too Legit to Quit*—stuck in my head.

By next semester, the foundation was set for our students. Time reveals truth, for it stops for no one. Ironically, not all teachers cared to improve at their craft, or accept our school's mission. I guess it was human nature. There will always be those unwilling to grow, and those who embrace mediocrity. We had a leader to lead the way, but would the people follow?

What are your thoughts about following tradition?

Are you open to change? If yes, how often? If not, what are the challenges?

_____

_____

_____

_____

_____

_____

_____

_____

_____

_____

_____

_____

_____

_____

_____

_____

_____

_____

_____

4

"You will give the people an ideal to strive towards. They will race behind you, they will stumble, and they will fall. But in time, they will join you in the sun. In time, you will help them accomplish wonders." - Man of Steel.

After the famous PTA meeting, some of the parents withdrew their children. Dr. J. was fine with it. Once they withdrew, he did not make it easy for the parent to re-admit their child back in school if things did not work out with their intended destination. Juice knew they would want to return once the receiving school denied their admittance. I suppose those parents believed that if they got their way at Bethune they could go somewhere else and do the same. That type of attitude never worked out in their favor. They needed something that would awaken them to the reality that not all schools operate under foolishness. In my assumption, I believed some of the schools in the district that were under African American leadership were permitted to operate in perpetual chaos. Yes, it was a generalization, but I thought my opinion was not far off the mark. It felt as though the needs of these schools were an afterthought compared to the higher performing schools. On the other hand, there were schools that steadfastly upheld their standards and policies. Anyway, the returning parent must have felt humiliated having to return. The one favorable thing to consider was that our supportive parents appreciated Juice for advocating for their kids who did the right things in school. Juice was a symbol of hope. He was doing something that had never been done here. He confronted the parents of the mischief-makers. The law-abiding students were stronger than the lawbreakers. They only needed adults in authority to support them.

The news of what happened at the PTA meeting spread like wildfire in the community. Based on the comments circulated, people liked our new direction of Bethune Middle. As a result, we received increased volunteerism and physical resources. Apparently, they believed in Juice's leadership. My intellectual eyes opened to the fact that things were getting done through the people. The better the relation

58

with the people the more things were accomplished. The community leaders eagerly came to the school to show their gratitude.

Over time, the storm-makers made their last-ditch effort to impede the new culture of the school. Maybe it was in their DNA to do so. Some people will muster up what little strength left to maintain their power. Having power is important but when in the wrong hands, destruction is inevitable. Thinking about that concept of not letting go directed me to Harold. To experience his present is to visit his past. Harold was a student who refused to let go of wrongdoing. He constantly did things to disrupt the learning environment. I hated to say it but when you saw him, trouble was nearby. He was a magnet for it. Harold had his share of suspensions, and truthfully, it was pleasant when he was not there. I knew my thoughts were not politically correct, but they were true. Truth needs to be spoken and lived more often.

Harold, who stood at 6'2", was a tall kid for 7th grade. He loved the game of basketball. The kid had potential, but his skill set needed developing. The basketball coaches worked with him to keep him eligible for the season, but it was all for naught. He was constantly in trouble both on and off the court. His behavior was more than the coaches could bear. I understood their frustration. There is something off-putting in a picture where the person helping you has more desire for achievement than the person being helped. Harold argued persistently with his teammates, on or off the court. He made basketball practice an unhappy environment. The perplexing part of this was his arguments were over trivial stuff. In his opinion, his favorite NBA team was the best team regardless of their last place standing. It sounds silly. Any person would assume that you were not the best team if you were in last place; however, once he started in Harold kept the argument going until things became a physical altercation. Every player has his opinion about what or who they like, but to argue and fight about it? Harold would do that. It was like he took everything personal. I figured that he needed some attention. It was obvious that maybe he was not getting enough love at home. I was baffled because whatever attention we shared did not seem to penetrate his hard exterior. Sometimes in life, a person chooses not to be loved regardless of how much love he's given. Unfortunately, Harold was that person.

The coaches believed that negative behavior can be changed through positive actions. Personally, I do not believe that a student is forced to do bad things when he is exposed to others doing good things. It becomes a choice and a student at this age can make a change in his behavior. His home life may influence one way but being at school presents a different atmosphere. I have not met a teacher who refuses to help kids when they show they want help. Kids do not understand that every negative thought, every negative act, builds a wall that becomes unmanageable to climb.

Along with the coaches, some teachers invested personal resources in Harold, but his unwillingness to cross over the bridge of destruction to friendship was a futile journey. He broke their trust and once it was broken, he could not earn it back. Tutorial sessions, clubs, and counseling sessions failed to reach Harold's inner goodness. He had to be academically eligible to play, so his teachers supported him, but whatever was inside was too much for him to overcome.

Harold did not accept the appropriate social etiquettes of society. A person must master working with people if they want to get what they want. The universal law of cause and effect is always in play. Everything we do in life has a consequence. Some people's philosophy is that they only help others when others help them first. I think differently. I like to think of service as fruit. A gardener plants seeds to produce fruit. When the fruit is ready it is harvested, ready for consumption. A person's service to others is the fruit that later returns through someone helping you. Mr. Archibald and Mrs. Fischer, our school counselors, worked with Harold. They held counseling sessions with him, but his rhino exterior was too tough to penetrate. Whatever this kid has experienced, it was deep rooted.

I recall an experience with Harold. During a class transition, he had a confrontation with a student that got out of hand. An office referral was written, and he was sent to my office. After reading the referral, I called his mom requesting a conference. Many things had transpired with Harold, and I felt it was time for us to meet in person. Mom gave a distant reply over the phone. I could hear the hesitancy in her voice. I imagined it stemmed from receiving so many telephone calls regarding his behavior. I could understand but I could not condone. I did not know how involved she was in his life, but it appeared that she did not have authority. Harold was at an age where she was no longer able to influence him to do right. I sympathized. It is easy for another to say what someone else needed to do. Often, people quickly say what they would or would not do, but they do not know until they are in that position. I believed that people could change, and believed his mother could turn things around, if she desired. However, my belief could do nothing for her; she needed to believe for herself.

Ms. Billingsley, one of Harold's teachers, wrote the office referral and sent him to my office. She sent another student with him to make sure he made it. Sometimes without an escort our babies detoured to another destination. After receiving the referral, I began his due process. I knew that I wanted to be thorough in this process to be helpful to Harold. Harold and I talked. He had the opportunity to tell his side of the story before I questioned him. He went into his defense of denial, "I didn't do anything." "I see," I replied. "The referral reads, "Harold stated 'I am tired of this motherf****n sh##!' Also, I read that you slammed the classroom door and caused the window in the door to break." He sat motionless and speechless. He never responded to my questions. I sent him out to sit in the waiting area designed for our students to wait until an administrator was available. We did not want students with discipline issues waiting in the public's view. We thought it would give our parents and community members the wrong impression. Kids have a way of entertaining when they know an audience is present. Anyway, he needed a moment to cool down so we could hopefully have an intelligent conversation.

I took the opportunity to visit Ms. Billingsley who witnessed the account. Also, Mrs. Ellis was present to see the spectacle. She confirmed Ms. Billingsley's story. I collected the information I needed and returned to my office to complete my business with Harold. "So, Harold, you denied saying, 'I am tired of this mthrf*#*in s**t' and slamming the door breaking the window?" "I'm telling you it wasn't me. The teacher is trifling and wants to see me get in trouble. She doesn't like me and always says that she will write me up for the smallest things." I had to ask, "What is trifling?" "It means tripping," he said. "Okay." He did not give me much information to support his defense. He continued to deny and blamed others for bothering him which caused his emotional outburst. He stuck to his story that the teacher was lying on him and wrote him up because she did not like him.

Eventually speaking with his mother, she agreed to come to the school. I shared the specifics of his infraction and his consequence, "Harold received an office referral for using profanity and breaking a window in a classroom door. A due process was completed, and we did not find anything conclusive to warrant his behavior. He will serve 5 days of out of school suspension." I heard the anguish in her voice as she pleaded for us to keep him in school. "Mom, I am no longer able to give grace. He tries to intimidate other students. He rejects the help from authority. His behavior has become atrocious and is unacceptable at Bethune."

Well, disappointing to say, his mom never made it to the school. I guess I should say that I was not surprised. I called her again. Mom didn't answer. I left a voicemail of his suspension and return date. Both mom and Harold would need to meet with me before re-admittance. There were some discussion points we had to cover before permitting his return.

I prepared a copy of his paperwork to be sent home with him and a copy mailed to his parent. I thought about Harold's potential. Continuously, seeing him make poor decisions was hard to swallow. His travels were on a dangerous rocky path. I was more concerned about his well-being than he was for himself. But like every person, child or adult, he had the power to make his own decisions. So often, people want to blame others for their lot. Yes, I knew bad things happen to people. I am not saying that lightly, but at some point, a person must take responsibility for his actions. Every person has the capability to aim for better goals. I have seen success result from people who made the decision to improve. There are people with helping hands, waiting to do positive things for those who choose to do right. Wait, I thought. I was sounding like Juice Jordan.

Officer Flowers, student resource officer, ended up taking Harold home when his mother did not show. I detained him in the In School Suspension holding room. We only prescribed ISS as a holding area for those who got into trouble and their parent was not able to pick them up from school. In those cases, we would request Officer Flowers give the student a ride home but only in emergencies. Dr. J. did not believe in providing ISS for kids to come to school and spend their time doing work for their wrongdoings. Honestly, most kids that went to ISS only created havoc, because most were not looking to change their ways. Juice understood that some principals used it to lessen their out-of-school numbers or to keep the kids off the streets. He believed that school resources were to be used on students who chose to make right decisions. Basically, they were the students who were in their academic classes.

I recalled one day during my campus rounds passing by a window to see three student bodies standing outside. Classes were in session which meant they were skipping. They ran as I approached the door. I guessed they thought I was going to run after them. I think some kids are brain damaged. I heard their laughter, but they did not know that I would have the last laugh. Besides, I would have been a fool to run in my beautiful Christian Louboutin. My shoes were expensive and not made for running. Besides, I knew the district office wouldn't pay for any of my damages. Instead, I called Officer Flowers and alerted the administrative staff to be on the lookout. The competitive side of me wanted to go after them. My common sense reminded me that it would be a matter of time before they would get themselves caught.

I have learned in my short time, those who do wrong will soon be found out and it does not take much effort to expose the truth. A person's actions often speak what he or she really is thinking. I made my way back to my office to look at the surveillance video. I informed Officer Flowers that I found the footage of the culprits. He confirmed they were Dash, Mookie, and Julio. They have just given me a reason to give them some vacation time. I magnified the still shot of the digital video. It indicated the time of day, date, and location. Technology is amazing. It would be used on their behalf.

I checked with each of their teachers of the class they were scheduled. I needed to confirm that they each took attendance. Great! They had. The students were marked absent. Apparently, they sneaked out of the building in between class change. It was the last period of the day. Tomorrow would be their day. I made the decision to corral them first thing in the morning.

That next day arrived and anxious, I made it a point to be at the facade when the doors opened to receive the students. I did not want to miss those characters. Dr. J. was at his post welcoming the students as they entered. It was a good thing the boys were not the first ones to enter. I needed that time to collect my poise. The flow of traffic was fluid compared to the beginning of the year. Our first semester was nearly completed. By now, I calculated about five percent of our difficult students had withdrawn or been expelled from the school. We collected extensive evidence on the students for tribunal. Going to tribunal and not accomplishing what you set out to do was a defeating experience for the staff. It is a sad thing to say but who really wants to see the student return and cause more mayhem?

Two of my class skippers entered. As our eyes made contact, theirs widened with shock. At that moment, they knew I knew. By their response, they must have forgotten our encounter from the day before. "I need for the two of you to go and sit in the office waiting area." "Why do we need to sit there?" they asked. I did not respond. About five minutes later, the third culprit entered the building. He saw me looking at him and ran out of the building. I called for Officer Flowers for his assistance in locating the student. Flowers said he had it handled.

I finished morning duty and went to my office to hear their story. The look on their faces, when I entered, told me that they knew judgment time was here. As we walked into my office they performed their denial speech. Of course, both claimed that it was not them. It was nonstop excuses from both. They talked too much for me and it started to annoy me. They talked so much that I had not even given the reason for calling them to my office. I guess in their mind they figured that if they concocted a good lie, I would be gullible enough to believe it. I was not sweating it. I had sufficient evidence. I thought about how disappointing it was to see these young men choose a path of trouble; even though, some say that it is a person's path that chooses them. The beauty in life is that every person has the freedom of choice. People always have the power to choose what they want or do not want. It is called free will.

I looked up their discipline file. Based on what I saw, they qualified for OSS. The act of skipping by itself did not warrant the suspension, but their prior offenses and leaving the campus added to the consequence. I called the boys' parents and shared that due to their action, they would serve out-of-school suspension. I was lenient on the amount of OSS days given since they did not run. However, the third culprit was a different case.

I later learned that the third student was dealing with some major issues, in and out of school. His trouble out of school were police related cases. Apparently, he and some others had burglarized some apartments in the area. Administration became aware after Officer Flowers caught the boy and ran a routine check on him. He had a warrant for his arrest. Officer Flowers informed me that he would detain the student until the police had the opportunity to collect him. Some kids mind cannot be changed from living that kind of life. I suppose the world will always contain those with a poverty mindset.

It did not take long for the police to arrive. When the students saw the police car, they knew what time it was, so to speak. They only wanted to see who was going for the ride. The boy's parent withdrew him from Bethune on the same day. The process of this happened so quickly. His charges were more serious than we thought. Most likely, they would detain him at the juvenile detention center until his court date. I thought about the pain his mom was experiencing. During the withdrawal process, I could sense the agony on her face and voice. I hated to see her having to deal with his issues, but he was her son. She told me that he was uncontrollable at home. People tend to reveal more when they are emotional. Hearing what she had to say was not a surprise. Even in her emotional state, I was not totally sympathetic to her situation. It took time for his behavior to reach the level of what he was doing, and that meant she had time to correct his ways during his early stage of life.

Later that afternoon Juice called me into his office. "I have two sets of parents that I am scheduled to meet. I want you present in both meetings. I need a second set of eyes and ears. The first appointment is scheduled to be here in 30 minutes. After each meeting, let us evaluate our notes." "Okay, sounds good to me," I said. I went to my office to clear my mind before going to the meeting. Ms. Bond paged me over the telephone intercom. "Ms. Knight, Dr. J.'s appointment is here. He's expecting you in the conference room." "I'm on my way," I responded. I thought about how quickly 30 minutes evaporates. Seemed like I just sat down to meditate. Anyway, it was showtime. I left for the conference room. I did not know what to expect from this meeting. I figured this would another opportunity to add to my experience. Unknowingly, this would be an indelible experience. As I entered, I glanced at this giant of a man. His hands were huge and meaty. His balled fist looked proportionally larger than the size of my head. His shoulders were muscle on top of muscle like that of a mountain range. I greeted everyone as I entered. The parent mumbled a response with a deep voice that echoed throughout the room.

Who is his child I thought? I took my seat as Dr. J. opened the meeting. Mr. Wilkins expressed his issue. Dad was not happy about how his son, Ralph, was being treated. Apparently, a situation happened last week. It seemed that Ralph convinced his dad that the reason for his failing grades was the fault of a teacher who did not like him. Hence, the teacher failed him. Like so many of our parents, Mr. Wilkins reacted immediately with aggression and without rationale. His idea of handling matters was to come to the school and straighten out the teacher and any administrator that got in his way. It was obvious that Dad was livid and took the word of his son before investigating objectively. The more he talked, the angrier he became. The inflection of his voice increased along with his profanity. "How in the f#*k can my son be mistreated by your teacher, and you allow this sh*# to happen. What are you going to do about this?" Dr. J. calmly picked up his radio and called for Officer Flowers to come to the conference room. Juice never responded to dad's question. He let the man continue. Mr. Wilkins's anger reached its boiling point that passed the point of civility. Telling him to calm down would have escalated him more. Dad's antics led to the pounding of the table with his burly fist. He got out of his chair with a hostile stance, yelling and pointing his finger at Dr. J. When will Flowers get here, I thought? This man needed to be removed. His aggression was strong. His eyes were deep red with saliva pooling in the corner of his mouth. Officer Flowers entered poised. He politely asked Mr. Wilkins to exit the room. I looked at the dad. His posture was not agreeable to leaving the room.

I can only guess that he was used to getting his way because of his size. Dad did not move. Officer Flowers reiterated his request. I looked at Juice. Calmly, Juice told Officer Flowers to remove him and escort him out of the building. A visible altercation was not what the parents and students needed to see. They have enough off campus drama to see.

Two other Student Resource Officers were in the area. They responded from a call by Flowers. I guess he had prepped them in advance of this dad's behavior. It was better to be ready than not. To help keep matters low key, the two officers entered through the back entrance of the school. The students in this community were more than familiar with the police. They knew something was taking place when they showed. It was an intense moment. I have seen Flowers in action and knew that he could handle himself without issue. I guess it was protocol for him in this situation to have back up. I suppose for law enforcement, it was not about ego but safety for the perpetrator and bystanders nearby. The other two SROs entered the conference room after Flowers. I saw the disgusted look on dad's face. "Gentlemen let's make this happen," he said.

Dad was a huge man, but the officers were not small men either. They were trained for this. I knew this was going to be ugly. This was a visceral moment for me as my heart raced. I could feel the shortening of my breaths when Juice said it was time for the two of us to leave the conference room. The men engaged in contact before we could completely exit the room. Juice quickly closed the door behind us. I could hear the banging and breaking of what sounded like wood. I distinguished the sound echoing off the cinder blocks as bodies banging against them. I could hear their muffled voices. It was soon that their words dissipated. Perhaps, the tussling of one against three was too much for dad. His words started off distinguishable but soon ended with the panting of deep breaths. The ego of a man sometimes must be tamed. The dad's ego led him to this dead-end moment, and now he had to pay for his product of pain, shame, and wrongdoing. The scuffle lasted for about 3 minutes before the door opened. I saw dad in handcuffs. He was banged up with red whelps covering his arms and shoulders. A tiny river of blood streamed down from his scalp to his cheek bone. His hair looked as though he just walked out of a wind tunnel. His gasps of breath were aggressive.

Juice motioned for the dad and the officers to stop. He told the man that he would pursue charges against him for his actions. "Your actions today is an example of the type of culture we choose not to have at our school. We no longer succumb to verbal threats or physical threats. Just so that you know. We completed the due process regarding Ralph's accusations. He was not truthful with you. Officers, please take him away." Dr. Juice concluded and walked away.

I understood Mr. Wilkins's anger regarding his son but wanting to force us to do what he wanted was the wrong way. Some parents believe that they can bully teachers and administration. Based on dad's actions, I get why his son felt like he had to lie. He did not want to receive that necessary butt whipping, but lying is not the way.

Flowers communicated to Juice that he was taking the dad to the police station. It was amazing to me how Jordan was calm throughout it all,
even when dad went over the edge. The event seemed surreal. I have never seen a parent act that way. Teachers may experience some verbal resistance, but for the most part, things wouldn't get turned up to the level of physicality. That experience opened my eyes. As crazy as it was, this experience added more in my leadership bag. I kind of felt as though we took one for the team. Meaning, we shielded a teacher from this person whose only objective was to bully. Administrators must support teachers so they can teach, and the students can learn. I thought about the student's perspective. I see why some students hate to go home, especially when living with an explosive parent. Anyway, right is right and wrong is wrong. Regardless of the home environment, a young person must learn to cope with his emotions to make appropriate decisions.

Dr. J. often reminded me that it is always a tragedy to see a young person choose a path of destruction and unfortunate to see adults doing the same. Adults are the model for the young. An impressionable child imitates the behavior of the adult, unless the child is consciously strong enough to transform his thinking to not follow the adult.

An antithetical thought interrupts. Some children are fortunate to use their parent's negative thinking as inspiration of how not to be. I smiled. A ray of inspiration filled me. Yes, with right thinking and support, a student can do great things. It just starts with a strong-willed mind to make that decision.

The end of first semester... Dr. Juice was not inhumane as some claimed. He rewarded the staff with a party. Juice often stated how important it was for a team to respectively work cohesively. A chain is as strong as its weakest link. A committee of teachers, staff, and community leaders worked to coordinate the event. The school's café was the party location which meant the décor would have to be elegant to hide the cafeteria feel. Fine dining cuisine with appetizers, entrée, and dessert was provided. Juice paid for a live band to entertain for the evening. I sneaked a peek at the event's menu. It was delectably done with Sambal Shrimp tossed in an Asian sweet-spicy sauce served with a ranch dip, Ahi tuna sesame peppered and lightly seared and served sushi-style with ponzu sauce, Smoked Brisket Crostini with Bleu Cheese and Wasabi Cream, Flash-fried Calamari with crushed red-pepper aioli sauce, and handmade vegetarian spring rolls. The dessert options were Banana Pudding Cream Cheesecake, Crème Brulee, and Death by Chocolate Cake made with Ghirardelli Chocolate. Reading the menu ignited my palate. An event of this magnitude should improve the teacher's morale.

Before his campus stroll, Dr. J. stopped with a question, "What are your thoughts about timing?" He walked away before I could answer. His ways sometimes were unorthodox. Anyway, I knew dealing with Dr. J. meant there is a lesson. His modus operandi reminded me of a hit-and-run. His question made me think. Knowing him, he would return for my answer.

Party night... The teachers looked amazing as they trickled in the building. It was beautiful to see the staff in their evening attire. I was pleasantly surprised. I almost did not recognize some of them. The ladies had their hair done and were wearing their beautiful dresses. The men were clean-shaven in their haberdashery. The night had a great feel to it. This was a night for pictures.

Dr. J. summoned me over the P. A. system to his office. He didn't have a smile on his face. Does he ever loosen up I thought? "Dr. J., it feels good to see the staff at this type of event, doesn't it?" I asked.

"Yes, it does. Unfortunately, on this great night you and I must grace one of our teachers with unpleasant news." "Tonight?" I perplexedly questioned. Juice explained, "Yes. There is an ethics allegation we must address. It has come to my attention about an hour ago that a teacher made sexual advances toward a male student. After conducting our due process, the evidence collected confirmed the allegations to be true. The Board has sent approval for his immediate termination. I know right now is not the best time, but we can use this opportunity to send a message to our staff that our actions speak louder than our words. Tonight, we must call him in and inform him of the Board's decision. I wouldn't be surprised if the boy's parent pursued charges against him or the district." "Who is the teacher?" I asked. "It's Mr. Thompson."

Dr. J. summoned him to his office prior to my arrival. Mr. Thompson knocked on the door. Juice invited him in and asked him to close the door behind him. Thompson took a seat. He had an uneasy look in his eyes. They shifted back and forth rapidly at Juice then to me. Juice asked, "Do you know why you were called to this meeting?" "No, I do not." Was Thompson's stare an attempt to pierce through me? I made sure to return the stare. I wanted him to know I would not back down. He refocused on Juice. "There has been a sexual allegation made against you. A committee completed their due process, and the result showed evidence against you. My position is to inform you of the allegation and the Board's decision." Thompson's eyes widened. I saw fear in his eyes for the first time that night. Juice shared the details, "We have evidence that you made sexual advances to one of your male students. The student first reported it to the counselor, which obligated him to report it to me. As the principal of the school, it is my responsibility to investigate. We found evidence for the Board to terminate you." Mr. Thompson sat silently and stared at the floor. It has been a long time since I was fired from a job, but I still remember that ill-feeling going through it. It was a summer job with the City of Atlanta Parks and Recreations. The embarrassment of having to leave the office knowing your colleagues are aware is…damn.

"Your action undermines our culture," stated Dr. J. "Is my termination immediate?" asked Mr. Thompson. "Yes. Officer Flowers will escort you out of the building. Please contact the human resources department to organize when you can return to collect your personal items. This meeting is over unless you have any questions?"

Mr. Thompson sat motionless and quiet. He wore a dejected countenance. I turned my thoughts toward the student and how he must feel. His life has been impacted because of Thompson's actions. Even though we were meeting with Thompson, the focus to me of this event was not about him. This was about the student. I anticipated he would transfer. How long has Thompson been dealing with this issue? Was this private from his colleagues? It was inexcusable for him to infect another person with this pain. I hoped the trauma was not too emotionally deep beyond repair. Would this leak out to the public? Juice reminded all parties that the meeting was confidential, but in theory, would it be?

Thompson stood up and slowly walked out of the office like a whipped puppy with a tucked tail. I had mixed feelings of anger and sympathy. What he did was inexcusable, but part of me wanted to forgive and the other part of me burned with anger for punishment.

My thoughts turned toward the welfare of our students. Some of them were living some tough life challenges. We have young adults with weak parenting skills who are allowing kids to raise themselves in this fast-paced mean and unforgiving world. This label I place on these weak parents are those who place priority on self above their child. A responsible parent takes a back seat to their selfish desires. I will not ever make light of being a parent. It takes great discipline for them to put their total energy into their child. A parent's quality investment in their formative years yields a fruitful result.

My parents instilled in me what I consider sound values. Both sacrificed their selfish wants for my success. It was not about giving me everything or making me feel entitled. They supplied me with the necessary fundamentals to be a positive contributor in this society. I was taught to respect authority. We had a dialogue regularly and because of those talks, I learned how to evaluate my thoughts. Our relationship was healthy in my eyes. I only wish that some of our students could see what a healthy parent-child relationship model looks like. Then maybe, more would have a better chance at succeeding.

It takes time to transform a mind from hopeless to hopeful. It can be done, but it will take a decision, desire, and discipline to make it happen. Successful people learn to construct, not destruct. They accept that they are given life to make a difference, not blend in with the majority. There's purpose in their creation. Purpose gives life meaning, energy, and fulfillment, and without it, one wanders aimlessly, looking for the why of their existence.

At Bethune Middle we strived to provide our students with a healthy model for social relationships. It starts with a positive self-image. A person will never rise above how he sees himself. Consider the analogy of a sports car that is designed to operate on 91 octane fuel. If the driver uses 87 octane fuel, over time it will underperform. The more he drives with the incorrect recommended fuel, the less his vehicle will produce its maximum performance. Over time, the car and the driver will acclimate to its sluggish performance. People, like machines, can underperform in the same method.

Dr. J. strategically created a conducive environment for our student and teacher growth. We have one mission and that is to improve our minds. Our aspirations are that our young people are productive in our communities. John C. Maxwell, a renowned author, states that "Leadership is influence; nothing more, nothing less." Denoted by his phrase, I consider our students as leaders who are actively influencing one another. The power of influence is magical from moment to moment and person to person. Teachers influence students and students influence teachers.

Teachers can sometimes underestimate their influence on their students with the power of connection to academically drive their students. The caveat here is that teachers must know their limit when it comes to student performance. Students are not robots but human beings who have emotions. To not acknowledge this so puts this person behind the "eight ball." Every movement of the instructor is valuable and must be respected when in their presence. Students observe how they enter a room and mimic their body gesturing. They listen to their word enunciations to imitate them. Teachers should be understanding when they see this. The student does not mean any ill will. They do so because that is their way of saying they like you. You have captured their attention. I recall when I first began teaching. I caught a student mimicking me and took it as an insult. I thought she was mocking me. Thus, I went over the top. I really let the student have it. I went a step further and called her parents about her disrespectful action. At the end of the day, I shared what happened with my teammate. Through our conversation, she explained to me that the student's action was a gesture of respect. I thought about it and later felt bad. I later apologized to the student for my ignorance. Now, looking back, I should have seen it sooner. Hey, there were times when I did the same by imitating my former principals.

I love to watch athletic events. I think teams provide the perfect platform for people to work together for the accomplishment of a goal. Successful programs understand how to plug their players into its system. I look for the player who displays strong confidence. His belief makes him unstoppable and oftentimes his actions inspire his teammates. My achievements were based on my beliefs of what I thought I could do. So, it is true that what you believe or disbelieve, your creative nature is unbiased. Your subconscious mind does its part to prove your belief. In comparison, the same principle occurs for non-athletic organizations. In his book called *Good to Great* by Jim Collins it analyzes this concept. His research concluded that Good to Great companies operate under a proven system. They have a confident, humble leader, the right employees, and a workable system. One quality that stood out to me was when an employee bought in to their leader, this employee took ownership in the system.

For me, taking ownership at Bethune meant being instrumental at providing a positive culture for the staff. The teachers had a right to be treated and respected as professionals. Great athletic coaches used practice time to prepare and train players for the potential obstacles they may encounter in a game. As administrators, we must provide the same service to our teachers. Coaches prepare their players on how to react in any given situation before the experience. As administrators, we must provide the same concept for our educators. Juice believes teachers should think like an administrator. As educators, we want our students to collaborate and constructively work through proposed issues, compromises, and practices for future endeavors in their careers, then we must do the same.

It is becoming easier for society to advocate against student competition. Personally, I do not think kids look at competition as a detriment. They accept it as a part of life, but the adults have made competition into this esteem-monster. Now comments are made that both winners and losers should receive a trophy for participation, not the win. If this is the case, why should there be a competition? Truthfully, a lack of competitiveness is a concept that does not apply in society or in our economic system. Students know it is a natural component in school, sports, recreation, and relationships. Maybe more time should be used to educate our students to be confident in their skills.

I think it is a wonderful thing for educators to be transparent with their students, with discretion of course. Things are so delicate in this age that anything from a teacher's mouth can easily be taken out of context. Even though I was cautious about what I said to my students, there were a few occasions when I let something inappropriate fly out of my mouth. It usually happened when frustration got the best of me. Teachers need to be able to teach, not be a counselor, or a parent to their students. The best practice is for teachers to be friendly to students, not their friends.

This administration supports our teachers by not condoning disrespect from students. We expected our students to comply with authority in the building and when the student didn't, the appropriate consequence was given. I caught myself having a dialogue in my mind. You would think it is a natural thing to serve students consequences for their misconduct, but that is not always the truth. Some schools allow students to wreak havoc in the classrooms and in the hallways. Letting students appear to be in control, or as I say, "letting students create their own agenda" is ludicrous. It sends out the wrong message to the students that follow the rules. As a teacher, I have had administrator's follow up on a student's office referral consequence was a "good talking to." The administrator's advice moving forward was for me to "pick my battles." That was such a deflating moment. How could I feel secure knowing that all students were not held to a standard, and having that uncomfortable feeling was when I doubted the leadership of my principals? For us here, the result we want for our students is to learn and like the process. I could sense they wanted more. Dr. J. was not about resting on laurels, being satisfied with a little taste of success. He wanted more and challenged the students, faculty, and staff for greater aspiration. The world admires and loves champions.

I rejoined the party festivities. My thoughts were heavy, and I needed lighter energy. The event with Mr. Thompson was weighty and Dr. J. saw it in my face. He stopped me and stated, "Life can do that to you." "What do you mean?" I asked. "Life can jolt you. Sometimes we do not realize just how much it impacts us until the tension becomes overwhelming. Your face and posture show your feelings. Once, a sage reminded me that the greatest man on earth could not address every issue and shoulder all disappointments of the people. As strong in nature this person was, there was a point when he had to get away to recoup his energy. Our bodies are limited." His statement gave me an idea. Boldly, my words exited my mouth, "Respect people, help them and understand them as best you can, but don't take ownership of their problem. If you do, it becomes yours. Every person is responsible for his own successes and failures."

"Helping people can define you. It is satisfying, but you must keep in mind to not lose sight of your mission. Helping means assisting, not doing the job for the person. Some people believe that others are at their disposal. Ms. Knight, keep in sight your aspirations and evaluate wisdom you receive." I smiled and went to the party. I received his words. I think the empathetic are impacted the most. They take on other's emotional state and run with it. Why? Do these people think it is their human duty? Afterwards, I immersed myself into the lovely setting. The lighting was quaint, and the decorum was romantic. The D.J. played a mixture of old school songs and new. The faculty and staff were having a wonderful time. This event was needed. It was a time for all to relax and reenergize for the upcoming days. There is a balance in life every person must keep staying productive while serving others. Looking around, to my surprise I saw Dr. J. rocking his head to the beat. Everybody at some point in life can use help.

I enjoyed myself at the party, but the time came to an end in the evening. I said my goodbyes and went on my way. While driving I received a call from Zakiya. She and I have been friends since our college days. A business meeting brought her to the city for the evening and decided to call to see if we could meet at *Arizona 14*, a sport bar to have some wings and conversation. I agreed to meet her there. Excitement filled me. Zakiya and I became close friends and have stayed in touch. Besides, I knew she always had some gossip that we needed to catch up on since we last met. Fortunately, the sports bar was near my house.

She picked the right spot for delicious wings and atmosphere. *Arizona 14* was a great spot to see famous people. Often, entertainers and athletes dined there. If you were into that kind of scene, this was the place. When I saw her, we screamed and hugged. It took us no time to dig into our gossip bag. As we talked, I glanced over at the flat screen on the wall. It caught my attention with Batman Begins playing. It was a captivating feeling that it drew my attention from Zakiya. Her voice seemed to fade into a muffled sound. It was one of my favorite movies that I loved watching. However, this was not the time nor place to do so. I made a mental note to watch this weekend in the comforts of my house. Right now, I need to refocus on Zakiya. "Hey girl, let me bring you up to date on job change.

The movie made me think about the need for a superhero. The people in need may not see him or her coming, but he or she appears at the right time. This superhero's presence gives you a sense of security, and his actions may inspire you. Give and it shall be given is a creed to live by. I thought about Dr. J. and how he lives by a strong moral code.

He is not one to proselytize. He did not consume your time trying to make you believe. Superheroes dedicate their life for the protection of the people. Dr. J.'s commitment to provide a quality education is evident. This reminds me of this heroic effort. What he would do if I bought him a black cape. My mind is silly at times; I grin.

As a leader or supervisor, do you ask yourself, "Whatever I ask someone to do, will this be a growth experience or merely more unnecessary work?"

_____

_____

_____

_____

_____

_____

_____

_____

_____

_____

_____

_____

_____

_____

_____

_____

_____

_____

How often do you ask yourself how you can take a coworker's issue and turn it around to find a hidden opportunity?

_____

_____

_____

_____

_____

_____

_____

_____

_____

_____

_____

_____

_____

_____

_____

_____

_____

_____

5

Jordan is not a person who did things without purpose. The release of Mr. Thompson was a statement sent to the staff. For Dr. J. there must be a purpose for greater good, or why do it? He wanted the staff to see Officer Flowers escort Mr. Thompson out of the building. The visual impact was more indelible than just hearing a rumor.

Juice lived by standards, and he expected nothing less from his faculty and staff. He considered no one is above the law. I have heard of where the bureaucracy is so thick that some leaders were slow at moving teachers through the transfer process. Obviously, a leader decides how fast he or she wants to act; especially, when acting too fast from their emotions. That is a sure way to kill your career. Looking at this from an administrator's perspective, he must consider the impact of his termination. Their employment is their livelihood. Think about how a family can be impacted by the disruption of their income. The emotional and psychological stress can weigh heavily on the family. The other side of the coin of this issue should be equally considered. This event can be tragic with a leader's actions being too slow, too fast or failing to act. All the choices are killers of the staff morale.

As a teacher, I would hear other teachers talk about the motives of leadership. They questioned as to why they were not taking action on certain issues. Ms. Nesmith, a colleague at my former school, would either miss multiple days of work during the week or come to work late. She always had an excuse for doing so. There were times when she would have to leave early. The other teachers would have to step up and cover for her. In the beginning, we were happy to step in to help. However, there becomes a time when enough is enough. She had a responsibility to carry out just as the others. Her behavior continued throughout the year. It was apparent that she didn't prioritize teaching. Eventually, her actions wore on us. We lost trust in her as a teammate. Her absences communicated to her students that she was not committed to them. There were moments when I would hear the students complain that she was never there. In their language that meant she did not like them. Dr. J. is not mercurial in his decisions. His diligence is thorough. His advice to the people who thought they were sneaky was that their nature would eventually expose their actions. There is no need to police them. The universe will do it for you.

The law of sowing and reaping is unstoppable. What a man sows, he shall reap. It is a universal law as is gravity. No matter how much a person believes he can fly, let him jump off a 10-story building without a parachute. Gravity will win, and I pity the fool who tries it.

Days later, Juice joined me on one of my campus rounds. I was surprised and pleased that he wanted to walk with me. These are the times when I have my opportunity to observe the classrooms and check on the barometer of the students. Really, it was a time to show my presence to the students and teachers. There is reassurance in consistency. It was a great opportunity for a teacher to inform me of any issues that needed to be addressed. Sometimes my face was enough to curtail an issue before it got out of hand. Today was a day that our students would be graced with us both.

"Ms. Knight, have I shared my story about how I became an administrator?" inquired Juice. "No, you haven't," I responded. He continued, "In the beginning of my career I had no intentions of becoming an administrator. The model of leadership I was under didn't inspire me to be on that echelon. I think the appropriate word for how I felt was disenchanted. I realized this clearly when I approached my grade level administrator for wisdom on how to become a better teacher and walked away with nothing. The guidance I received was to attend some developmental workshops. Professional development has its place, but there is an awesome exchange when it involves physical interaction between people. The workshops I attended were informative but had that element of no connectiveness. You know what I mean, you attend and leave inspired. Later, you forget what it was you learned."

"There is value when you have consistent interaction and support. Some history and culture are shared. Ages ago, information was shared through stories. There was a connection between the person telling and the one listening. But now, that option is extinct. I think guiding a person to read a text or attend a workshop works for some, but the human element of interaction is missing."

"This diminished my belief in that leadership. I felt I was not growing. I loved teaching and being in the classroom. I felt I had more power being in the trenches with the kids than being in administration. I found there is positive energy being around the students more than being around bureaucratic adults. Some of my friends and family members thought my vision was narrow because I was not aspiring to be in administration. I was okay with it. It was their opinion. I just did not want my reason for leaving the classroom to be because of wanting to get away from grading papers, calling parents, or classroom disruptions. These reasons did not make sense to me. Even as an administrator, you interact with parents and deal with student behavior. I knew my responsibilities would increase from the 100 students in the classroom to an entire grade level. In my mind at the time, I didn't see an advantage of being at the next level."

"My reason for becoming an administrator became apparent when I grew tired of the nonexistent leadership I was under. It frustrated me that leaders were not doing the things necessary to support their students. Students were begging for the people in authority to clean up their school from students who didn't value education. Yes, I was sick and tired of my leaders blaming the teachers for poor student performance. Most importantly, I was dissatisfied with seeing apathetic students not care about learning or destroy the learning environment of those who wanted to learn. This was a battle that I knew I had to fight, and it was not going to get better by me complaining. So, I decided to become part of the solution."

After hearing his story, I reflected on myself. I noticed as we entered the classrooms, the students looked perplexed. I think they were more curious than excited to see us come in together. When kids do not like something, they will let you know. I think most kids want approval from the adults, even in their adolescent years. Sometimes they put up an aggressive fight to be autonomous and private, but there is still a part of them that desires the adult to notice them and give them their approval. A couple of the students greeted Dr. J. and me. Our inspection was quick in each classroom. I found myself wanting to excavate more of his story. "Tell me more." He continued, "It took me time to recalibrate my thinking. When I was first promoted to administration, I entered thinking that I would gain leadership skills from my principal. Quickly, I saw that he was not the model I wanted to follow. Well, let me state it another way. By observing his methods I learned what not to do. I struggled in my early years knowing that I could not adopt his style, and worse for me was that I didn't have a mentor. Reality sunk in that my stay at his school would be short." "Really?" I inflected. "Thus, I started seeing hints that he was looking to replace me. He sensed that I wasn't a faithful follower in his system. As much as possible, he made it uncomfortable for me. Subtle comments were made public about what additions he needed for the school, which were my responsibility. Hence, my intuition sensed that my shelf life was short. Over time, he increased my duties with a shorter time frame to complete. Meetings were held without my knowledge, and often the leadership team voted on things without my input. I did not need an 18-wheeler to hit me."

"So, he used underhanded tactics to make it appeared you were inadequate at your job," I stated. "There were no secrets between us. I knew and he knew, but what could I do? He held the position of authority. I had common sense to know that consuming time to combat his methods were a waste of my time and effort. Besides, my dad once told me the worst thing an employee can do is try to prove his boss wrong, especially in front of people. I must admit, after a couple of years of being there, I developed a poor self-image. Often, there were many days that I struggled being at work."

"One day, a grandparent of a student approached me. He asked how I was doing and how things were going for me at the school. I gave him the typical answer of okay. To this day I can recall his words. It was life a changing moment for me. "Mr. Jordan, you are unique with purpose on this earth that no one can accomplish but you. Until you can vision what it is, you will not feel satisfaction in this profession or your personal life. You will wander aimlessly and be unhappy. Find your purpose, for it is your responsibility. It is within you and only you can uncover it. I believe you already know what you need to do. People are waiting on you." He shook my hand and wished me a wonderful day.

"I couldn't get what he said out of my head. When I arrived home, I thought more about his message. The peculiar thing was that I never saw him again. After meditating on his words, I knew I would dedicate my life to changing student lives the right way. I made a vow to fight for students who valued rules, standards, and education. I knew it would not be easy but sacrificing oneself is never easy. Mr. Joe Clark *Lean on Me* was my inspiration. I made it my mission to turnaround underperforming schools. No longer could I accept working in an environment of mediocrity. Opportunity was plentiful. That same year I applied for a principal position in the district. Surprisingly, I was given an opportunity at a middle school. I say surprisingly because I was sure my current principal would impede my transfer. What I didn't know was that I had support from outside influential supporters."

"My attitude changed. My focus became laser sharp, and I developed my system even while under the current leadership. It took some years to perfect my system. Of course, I made my mistakes, but I learned from those mistakes. Quickly, parents started to support me, and their support strengthened me. As our results improved, more supporters joined. Newton's Law took over as an object in motion stayed in motion. The school experienced major decreases in classroom referrals, improved academic performance, and increased parental engagement. I stayed true to my standards by upholding policy, regardless how insistent a student or parent resisted. The faculty saw that I would not compromise on policies. Ms. Knight, you will find out who is on your side when you take a stand for something. Changes in our environment meant a change in school culture. The students were not the problem. They adjusted to the environment presented. However, the adults are a different story."

"How long did it take for the new culture to take effect?" I asked.

"One day, a business owner in the local community scheduled a meeting with me. I remember I was at the end of my second year as principal. I figured he was soliciting for the school to buy his product. It turned out he was not. He met with me to give a personal thank you for the school's efforts at turning things around for the students. The perception of the school in the community had improved. He stated that the community leaders could see the attitude improvement in the kids. The students seemed hopeful and excited about attending school. Sometimes it is not easily visible to see change when you are amid the process, so he felt obligated to inform me of the good news. He encouraged us to keep doing what we were doing. His confirmation hit me square between the eyes. After hearing his statement, I let nothing stop me."

I asked Juice, "Why are some schools willing to stay in their substandard state?" Juice responded, "There is major money in this industry. With the advancement of teacher training and technology, our schools should not be experiencing what I call an "urgent state" of decline in student performance. Obviously, we know that something is not right. Education has more professionals with master and doctorate degrees than ever, so our field should not be in a crisis with our students. In this capitalistic society, money is supplied to and made from programs that are broken, and we can agree that this educational system is broken, can't we? Also, consider another variable, the parents. Parents are the captain of this ship. When they understand the power they have as a collective group, they can direct quality education at the schools. In poor performing schools, the parents who do get it usually end up withdrawing their child. Most send their child to a private institution, but they can find out that a private school is not a panacea for quality education. Even private schools cannot guarantee the best education. They have issues in administration, parents, and students like public schools. A quality school is decided by its leadership and teachers. The way things are progressing in public education, it is going to take something equivalent to a nuclear explosion to redirect it on the right path." Dr. J. was called on the radio to address an issue in the office. Continuing my rounds, I reflected over his story. Juice was not a person who told stories just for the fun it. He wanted you to surmise the moral, but isn't that what great teachers do?

As time moved forward, I needed to prepare for our faculty meeting. Faculty meetings are interesting to me. It is a moment for teachers to observe the mannerisms of others they do not see daily. Besides, it was a day that we all loved, facetiously speaking. I love to humor myself. It keeps me balanced and rejuvenated. Juice gave me the responsibility to create the agenda. I made sure it was concise. Mrs. Bond printed the copies for the staff.

I opened the meeting with the reading of our school mission. Dr. J. took it from there. "I want you to be reminded of the students who no longer attend Bethune. It was their choice. I know the parents of those students do not care to hear this, but they were the enablers of their child's behavior. It is the guardian's responsibility to teach appropriate public behavior. Parental influence is powerful, especially in their child's formative years. Often, I wonder if our parents are aware that they are a powerful entity when it comes to education. Collectively, they can create major change for the right reasons when they ban together."

"Over the years, I've conducted a study on the success of the recognized private and public schools. I looked for trends in their students' grades, standardized test scores, and any parental reviews. The common qualities I found were the following: students were happy about going to school, parents actively volunteered at their school, teachers and parents formed allied relationships, and the administration made sure staff had quality teaching resources."

I observe the facial reactions and body gestures of the teachers as Dr. J. made his statement. Some heads were nodding in agreement while others sat with a blank stare. Juice continued, "We have been successful with what we called the Phase I Initiative. Phase I involved introducing the new culture. It was about helping the students to know our expectations, rules, consequences, and standards. The change started with us, the adults. We had to model for our students and show that we adhered to the rules. The students who attend Bethune now see that our culture offers an environment of freedom. We want our student body to feel comfortable in their space. Now that we have established a foundation, Phase II is next." Some looked around the room in a quandary. I could hear some whispers asking, "What is this Phase II?"

"Phase II involves getting our parents positively engaged in the school. It is going to take you, the teachers, to encourage and support your parents. Our students, when appropriately encouraged, will be helpful in this process. Parents listen to their child when he or she talks about their likes. Parents love to see and hear their child happy. That means they have one less thing to worry about when it comes to them. We have an open house event scheduled. The office will mail out invites to our parents. I need for all staff to save-the-date. Let us make our numbers in attendance strong. We want our parents to be a presence in our school. Once we get them here, we can educate them on how they can best assist us."

Some of the teachers looked like they got it and others looked hesitant. "The staff culture we've created cannot sustain phonies. Quality staff is like cream that rises to the top. Phase II includes exposing teachers who are not the best for this environment and assisting them to a more conducive environment. Unfortunately, we have had some teachers to blaze this path. However, there are more to follow." Juice didn't elaborate on his comment. He shifted the topic and gave the teachers their room assignments for workshop training. He ended the meeting, and the teachers went to their respective destinations. I could not help but think, were the teachers wondering who are the chosen?

I once heard it said that there are three kinds of people in the world. One type is the person who does not know what is happening. Second type, is the one who was asks what is happening? The third type is the person who makes things happen. That thought took me to the quote on Juice's office wall stated by Carly Fiorina, CEO, Hewlett-Packard in 1999. It reads, "Every experience in life, whether humble or grand, teaches a lesson. The question is not if the lesson is taught, but rather if it is learned."

I pondered further on who would be the selected. My thought shifted to my relationship with the students. That was more important to me than a teacher's transfer. Often, credible students are a practical resource of information on what is happening in the trenches. Of course, one cannot believe everything they say. One must be sagacious.

Something to think about: Telling others most likely isn't drawing in the people to do; however, asking questions can get people to think in the direction you would like them to go, which puts you in a position of strength.

Why is it important to not give people the solutions to their problems, but encourage them to think about their solutions?

_____

_____

_____

_____

_____

_____

_____

_____

_____

_____

_____

_____

_____

_____

_____

_____

_____

6

"Everything is possible for him who believes." – Jesus.

Juice summoned me into his office and handed me a DVD. Curiosity filled my mind as it touched my hand. I wanted to look at it that moment, but I had something I needed to handle. I took it and dropped it off at my office. The matter was handled before returning to my office. I was curious about what was on the disk. I sat down to view the tape while admiring the 55-inch smart LED screen mounted on my wall. Sweet! I popped in the DVD and leaned back in my chair. I was in that kind of mood. I thought how nice it would be to dim the lights and snack on some extra butter popcorn chased with a Coke. Reality set in as I glanced down at the stack of office referrals on my desk. I heard the voices of Mr. Thorn, our Health teacher and Mrs. Linda, our 6th grade English Language Arts.

I pressed the remote menu button for the date and time. December 19th was the date, and the time was well after school hours. Mr. Bus, head custodian, shuts down the building at 6:30 P.M., unless there is an after-school event. Closing the building meant for all teachers to be out of the building. The time on the tape read 7:30 P.M. This really got my attention. Hmm I thought.

They knew the halls had video cameras, right? This is the kind of stuff you would see on a reality show. Evidently, discreet was not part of their arrangement. Both were married but to different spouses. The more I reflected, the more I recollected some of the coincidences of seeing them together. They were not overtly chummy at work, so apparently, they were cool at how they hid things. Watching the video, I could see that Thorn used the male teachers on Linda's hallway as his cover. He would go and fellowship with them and when the opportunity presented itself, he sneaked over to Mrs. Linda's room. As they entered her classroom, he gave her a gentle kiss on the back of her neck and patted her ass. OMG! This was incredible. They continued into her classroom. My, my, my as I shook my head. Lust can lead a person into a world of trouble. I guess they felt their burning desire for each other needed answering. Feelings like that often clouds logic. Thinking with your head never lies but making decision with the heart will get you into trouble. My mind imagined they were people caught on a strong ocean wave, and at some point, they tried to swim back to shore, but the current was stronger. It pulled them further out to sea until the shore disappeared. Hope was lost and no return accepted. Here they were. Did they consider how the narrative would end? How would it end? I could only guess.

Some claim what a person does in their time is their business and shouldn't be judged for it. What about the employer's viewpoint? It is the organization's accountability to respond to inappropriate behavior. An employee must consider their behavior on and off the premise as it reflects the organization. Regardless of the state of education, educators must maintain a credible reputation. Power in the hands of the immoral brings destruction. Ethically, there is no room for sordid deeds. How would I address this matter if I were the principal? I knew strong consequences were applicable. The video is damaging evidence and sexual misconduct is enough to revoke their certification. I was not sure how that worked. I only knew I never wanted to be the person in that spotlight.

I was surprised that I had not observed this sooner. Sometimes, it is easy to overlook the obvious when it is right in front of you like when looking for misplaced car keys. It is amazing how you could go through your entire house and not find your keys. If you don't find them immediately you may become frustrated to the point of giving up looking. It is then you finally relax and notice the keys sitting right in front of you. Something like that can mess with your mind. You question yourself on how you missed them in the first place.

I made my way to the conference with Juice after finishing the tape. I asked him how he became aware. "When you want to be in tune with your surroundings, the key is to not make a concerted effort to see things. Learn to relax in your environment. The more you relax, the more things appear. I do not have to go looking for it. Did you know that most athletes destroy their careers by doing things off the court than in a game? The truth always comes to the surface. It is like the athlete who did not address an issue privately in its early stage, and because he did not, it is likely that it will become public knowledge. Consider this case; the video exposed them, right? Had they been strong enough to curtail their lust in the early stage they would not be in this position. Now, I must address this, and it may go public. When I say public, I do not mean we are going to announce it to the public. No, we will uphold our duty of confidentiality. I meant that eventually others will know something because they are at a stage where it will impact their employment. Please, keep in mind our Phase II process."

"So, what's next?" I asked. "Formal action had to be taken with unpleasant consequences. I had apprised Human Resources of this issue and after an awaited decision, it was approved that both were to be released from their contract. The H.R. department would inform the Board of Ethics, and the Professional Standards Commission division will determine if any certification revocation is required. A mark on their record is damaging and could hinder future employment in education. Truth be told, I would not be surprised if both had difficulty acquiring a future teaching job. Their indiscretion comes at a huge price. Not only will it impact their employment but think about their marriages and families. Also, how will the community react to this?" asked Juice. "Wait, what does the community has to do with this?" I asked. "The public is hungry for gossip and never understands when it comes to these issues. People run fast with the negative news, creating hyperbole, but the contagion will not start from us. The news media thrives on this type of material. They feed the voracious social media appetite." "Okay," I murmured to myself while walking out of his office, shaking my head. "By the way, you didn't raise the question regarding Mr. Bus." "What do you mean?" I asked. "Do you think he was aware of them staying late?" Juice asked. "Now that you've brought that to me attention, he must have known," I responded. "He'll probably say that he was minding his own business and the two were consenting adults. Now ask yourself, what wrong did he commit in this situation?" "Well, anyone who stays after unapproved hours should have been reported," I retorted. "He did not, and now he must answer for it. Obviously, he would have been free of this mess had he said something to me when it first occurred however, too much time has passed for his excuse to be valid."

I knew what Juice was saying was correct. The dark side wants the people in authority to close their eyes to their wrongdoing. Those in authority cannot. We are talking about lack of character when those in authority turn their head regarding this matter. The masses need the law-abiding citizens to claim their rights in authority and be accountable in the power given to them. The Hooligans call those who tell snitches; but they use this tactic to intimidate. We cannot allow them to lead. Dr. J., nor I subscribed to that practice. Doing so would mean not supporting the ambitious to infect the world with productivity, excellence, and goodwill.

What type of consequence will Bus receive? It was then that Juice called him over the radio to come to his office. Upon his arrival, Juice did not waste time getting to the nature of this issue. He shared with him his negligence of duty pertaining to Linda and Thorn. Dr. J. reminded him that it was his duty to inform him. I could sense a level of emotion rise in the man. The whites of his eyes turned pink. There was a spooky feeling looking at them. Juice continued, "Based on your actions, the Human Resources department passed down its decision to terminate you." By the scowl on his face, I thought he would come across Juice's desk. The constant tapping of his hand on his leg caught my eye. I could tell this event blindsided him. Juice completed our business and dismissed him.

"Mrs. Linda and Mr. Thorn were next," stated Juice. As we waited, I thought about our meeting with Mr. Bus. He gave Juice his argument on why he should not have been punished. Juice reminded him that it was his responsibility to supervise the premises and that he had a duty to inform Dr. J. of issues, small or large.

Officer Flowers was called to Juice's office. He walked Bus to his car and watched him drive away. Bus was angry but was his anger directed at Juice or himself. Dr. J. collected all keys from him and told him that his things would be boxed and brought to the front office for pickup. I could sense that Juice was careful not to agitate him further. In heated moments, cooler heads prevail. When it comes to a person losing their employment, emotions are predictably high with unpredictable reactions.

People know the difference between right and wrong. Firing a person is never enjoyable, but before it gets to that stage, correction comes in various intensities. It starts off as low-level and often private, but when the correction is not accepted, the correction intensifies. When a child does something inappropriate, his parent will gently correct and redirect them. The correction may be as simple as a nod of the head, shaking of the finger, or a cutting of the eyes as to say "no." A similar process applies to adults. In the beginning, correction for an adult can be something as a simple private reminder. However, if the unwanted action continues, the correction will intensify with a high probability of it going public. Public awareness invites outside entities to get involved in your business. Unfortunately, we are in an age where the news is an appetizer for gossip. In the case of Mr. Thorn and Mrs. Linda, their indiscretion reached the public stage. Both had ample opportunities to stop but did not. They challenged fate and lost. It was time for justice to step in and render its judgment. Juice and I met with Thorn. It went just as thought. Officer Flowers escorted him out. Of course, this was good experience as I made my mental notations.

Juice called for Mrs. Linda. This meeting was a memorable event for me. He sent a paraprofessional to cover her class. I recalled how she entered the office with a look of bewilderment. I suppose I would have had the same look if I were called to the principal's office. I think it is the unknowing of why you are called that makes you worry. I could hear the nervousness in her greeting. Juice reciprocated the greeting and directed her to take a seat. "Mrs. Linda, let me get to the point. Do you have any idea why I asked you to come?" "No, I do not," answering with hesitancy in her voice. "An allegation has been made about you having sexual relations on this campus. Because of this serious allegation we were required to investigate. We viewed the video footage and saw the evidence. Your action is a breach of district policy; because of this, you shall receive a termination from your contract." At that moment sadness fell upon me. It was sad to see her in this position. There was an emotion that moved me that did not happen with Thorn. She never spoke a word as the tears welled up in her eyes.

I saw pain in her countenance as the tears overflowed her eyelids like water overflows a sink. The stream of her tears emotionally touched me. I handed her a tissue. I think the gravity of the situation became reality. Seemingly, an uncontrollable flow of tears came. This time I handed her the box. "Do you understand what has been said to you?" asked Dr. J. She nodded her head to say yes. "Mrs. Linda, may I ask that you verbalize your answers." "Yes, I understand" she answered.

Juice explained to her the protocol to be taken in this situation. "After we conclude, Officer Flowers will escort you out of the building to your car. You will need to contact the human resource department for the signing of your separation. I believe the Board of Ethics may be informed of your actions if H.R. decides. If applicable, the Professional Standards Commission will decide if your teaching certificate will stay active. Regrettably your loss will impact on your students' progress. Do you have any questions?" Mrs. Linda responded, "No, I understand." "Do you have any questions?" asked Juice. She verbalized, "No."

Juice did something for Mrs. Linda that he had not done for the others. He took time to console her. "Mrs. Linda, it pains me to see you experience this. I think you have the potential to become a great teacher. Having the right mentor could have supported you in making the right decision. Regardless of this outcome, you can turn things around, but it starts with the right thinking. Just know that when you have the right thoughts, the right actions will come. Does this make sense?"

"At this juncture, it's going to take courage for you to turns things around. Did you hold a negative self-image? What caused you to not trust yourself and to trust Mr. Thorn? The truth is that you are the only person who can love yourself. I am concerned for your well-being. You have so much to offer this world, and it is waiting on you. Your narrative to this world is your life; whatever you do, please do not place a period on this moment but a comma. For this is just a moment in your story, not the end. I do wish you the best."

Why did he take the time to console her? Linda's act of

indiscretion will negatively impact her teaching career. My mind was spinning with questions. Juice was to the point with the others. He did not add any extra like he did with her. Regardless of their mistake, I believe it was his wisdom to identify people with good character. I did not know the answers, but that was my conclusion on the matter. There is power in the person who reaches out to help another. How often do you hear about a leader doing what he did?

Some of the negative comments said about Juice Jordan flashed into my mind. Having the experience of being in his presence showed me those comments weren't correct. The law of assumption is strong in the human mind. It is remarkable how a person who does not know you can spread false accusations based on how they feel about you. I guess it is human nature. Because of how Juice does his job, he is easily misunderstood. It is the way the world works. If you are not a member of the group with power, you are considered the adversary, the misunderstood, or the unwanted. Working with Juice I understand why he has been called a superhero. He doesn't compromise his standards; he does care about people. I saw from his actions with Mrs. Linda that he cared, and I believe that is what people need from others.

Dr. J. reminds me of the eagle. An eagle's flight is high and solo. Their flight is higher than any other birds. The eagle is a fierce, majestic hunter. I took a moment of gratitude for having the opportunity to work with him. It is amazing to see how people judge others based on limited information. Dr. J. was personable when you allowed him to be. It is a leader's responsibility to know their people, and the people should have the ability to reciprocate the action. There is a two-way street regarding this subject. Sometimes, people must be friendly and reach out if they want to receive the same in return. Either way, Juice's actions were not based on how others thought he should do it. The thing I have learned is that he helps those who want to be helped.

Reaching out to Mrs. Linda is my evidence. Juice touched my heart. My emotions were almost overwhelming. I knew I did not want to cry in front of him or Mrs. Linda. I needed to be strong in front of both for my benefit. Afterwards, Mrs. Linda continued to cry. It was a low-level cry. Dr. J. sat with her for an extended time and talked.

Eventually, she stopped. I noticed that her eyes were trained on him. It was a magical moment to see. There are few moments in life when a person witnesses a magical moment and when you do, you must truly appreciate it. Part of me was empathetic to her situation. I thought about the sadness of her being taken advantage of by Thorn, but the other side of me considered the fact that she consented. When we finished, Mrs. Linda hugged Juice.

As I always do, I took time to evaluate our meeting. How often would you see an employee shake hands or hug the person who fired you? Mrs. Linda was released yet gave him a hug. Who does that? On her way out, Juice opened the door. I recalled her response, "Nobody has ever talked to me in that manner. I am unsure how to describe it, but your words reached me. Dr. J., thank you." She turned and walked away.

Later that evening, I stopped off at Saks Fifth. Today's events caused me to think about shoes. Shopping is one of my pastimes. I love the latest fashions. The time was late, and I could only visit one store. I evaluated my day as I shopped. My low point experience was the emotional feeling of seeing the release of Mrs. Linda; yet the high point of the day was witnessing Mrs. Linda rise from her emotional abyss. I was astounded how the same event contained both my low and high points. I saw a man whom most seem to judge unfairly, as a person who took the time to help a fellow human. My thoughts were heavy. The store traffic was light due to the time. I looked at my watch, and it was time to head home. Tomorrow is a long day. A faculty meeting is scheduled.

The next day…

The faculty meeting. Dr. J. relishes any opportunity for staff edification. Putting myself in his shoes, I understand how great leaders focus on strengthening their team through proper training and education. How else can we expect to be the best in this profession without it? Juice never settles for an incompetent staff. Training is a requirement for everyone, including him. I recall a session that focused on improving our current state. The agenda item focused on the essential question of how can we make our school more effective? All brainstorming ideas were challenged with two questions. Why are we doing this? And is this the right thing to do?

Juice opened the meeting with the essential question. We jumped in by dividing the staff into groups of four. Each group had a large tablet sheet and markers. In the center of the sheet the group wrote the essential question. Each group had the option to write or illustrate their answer.

I took the time to make my way around the room. I wanted to listen in on their conversations. Some groups created a web map formation, and others used the circle map formation to illustrate their answer. One of the groups posed their questions on their web. *How is effectiveness denoted and how is it visible in our school? Do we have the right personnel in the right positions for us to be effective? Is our staff getting quality training to make us better educators? What checkpoint dates do we have in place to keep us on track? Why do we want to be more effective as a school? How do our parent stakeholders assist us at being an effective school? Is our administration effective at teacher support and student-parent accountability? Do we have an open platform for the faculty and staff to voice their professional views without any repercussions? Are the teachers given sufficient time to produce quality work?* All work would be collected, recorded, with results later shared with the staff.

I thought Juice's actions showed trust in his staff, that we could elevate our school to higher heights. It was obvious that his leadership wasn't about micro-management. At that moment I paused...he didn't micro-manage. Organizations that recognize they are professionals know that this style drives them bananas. It causes a staff to be less transparent with their duties. Let this truth be told. Micromanaging is ineffective and shows weakness in the leader's ability to influence and trust.

Our time passed quickly. Juice closed out the meeting. "You've experienced something that many schools have not, nor will ever. You have participated in a session where the faculty could openly ask questions without any negative consequences. Some principals believe their staff should not question the existing process, but asking questions is right. Questions challenge an organization. The problem with an insecure leader is that he or she takes those questions as a personal attack on their leadership. This person asking the questions can be perceived as a troublemaker, or a non-team player. However, great leaders know that professionals cannot grow if they are not given the freedom to question the status. It takes a confident leader to empower his or her staff, to encourage them to question and explore possibilities for growth. Query is a required process in growth. A school is only as great as its teachers. What we did today is something that we will do periodically. Questions have been around since man has been on this earth. It is too bad that organizations have gotten away from the most effective way of learning. Keep in mind that there are two things that come out of a person's mouth, aside from bad breath, declaratives and questions." The staff laughed. It was good to hear their laughter.

"A statement tells, and a question causes us to think. Let me prove how powerful a question can be. Each person has what is termed an "answer reflex". When you are asked a question, this mechanism causes you to answer. If I ask you what you had for breakfast, you may not verbally answer, but I am sure in your mind you answered. Sometimes, the question can be more important than the answer."

"In regard to this workshop, your questions will be compiled and sent via email. Take a moment to peruse. Hopefully, the work you will see may cause you to move to action. Feel free to respond with feedback regarding the data. If constructively received, your questions can help give us greater efficiency in our future meetings. Please accept this challenge that our questions are for improvement, not blame. In the right frame of mind, they will persuade you in changing your thinking with the goal of making us better and stronger. My intention is not to sound pessimistic, but I realize a small percentage of you will continue to stay unwilling to experiment and change. If we want our students to become better at questioning, we must do the same. Let us encourage ourselves how to think. I thank you and make it a great evening."

After Juice's departure, some stuck around to continue their weighty conversation. One group traded thoughts on the questions they posed in the workshop. I reflected my thoughts on today's meeting. I witnessed a platform that professionals could build on. My eyes wandered to my watch. As interesting as it was to listen, it was time for me to leave. It was a long day and exhaustion was getting the best of me.

I gathered my things. I asked myself how can we get all teachers to buy into this approach? Also, how can our teachers encourage the students to question given concepts and learning targets? Reflection is a powerful tool in learning and most people do not use it to their advantage. During the early stage of life, a child is inquisitive about many things. I saw some research quote that the average four-year old asks about 300 questions a day, but the average college student only asks 20. Kids will ask question upon question. In the beginning, a parent is overjoyed when their child can speak words. Ecstatically, the parent encourages the child to talk more, then one day the child asks that powerful 3-letter question. Why? Their inquisitive nature forces them to ask why. They ask things like, "Why is there light outside?" The parent answers and the child quickly follow with another why? However, somewhere in the child's journey, he or she can encounter an adult that quells his or her organic nature. Adults can bark out to a child to stop asking so many questions, without regard for what it does to the child. The adult's frustration can thwart the development of their children in learning. Frustrating actions convert that once beautiful chatter of child talk and questioning into lack of organic expression. How does one learn if he is not permitted to ask?

Generations of adults are uncomfortable publicly when it comes to asking questions. It may take a little while for the child to reach their threshold, but a child will build an emotional wall. Add the ingredient of their classmate's ridicule to this recipe and the drama can become trauma. Peers can be cruel when it comes to a student asking questions in the class. A person's environment influences the behaviors of the child. So, a positive home and school environment is critical. If the habit of not asking questions is normal at home, how can it be expected differently at school.

Collectively, I was feeling good about our direction as a school.

Specifically, with the rate of progression. That afternoon's session was a grand slam. Putting together a championship program takes time. At least most of the staff were onboard. For the rebellious, the stagnant, and the uninspired teachers who were there, they were given the opportunity to change but needed to be encouraged to transfer.

Things were rolling smoothly. In this profession, I know what it means to count my blessings when things are calm. Storms are ever present even if the skies are clear. It is a matter of time before it comes. Case and point. Dr. J. asked me to look at some data he collected from a profit and loss sheet. I mulled over the numbers which looked okay to me. Nothing stood out of the ordinary. I returned the sheet to Juice and stated that it looked satisfactory to me. He gave me a thank you as he exited the office. Mrs. Bond came by to inform Juice that he had a phone call. What I didn't know then but later found out was that phone call he received was his confirmation of evidence for the P&L report. Reflecting, I thought about what he wanted me to see. Knowing Juice, there was a lesson in this. I grabbed my scheduler of what I needed to handle. Things have been operating smoothly, so if a storm was coming, what would it be?

Days passed since then. Dr. J. called over the intercom for me to come to his office. I finished what I was doing. On the way, I heard Mrs. Bond page for Ms. Simmons, our music teacher. Ms. Simmons is a veteran at Bethune, a fixture I call her. She had that 1960s look with a hair style that reminded me of the librarian. Her pink cat-eyeglasses were unforgettable. She could be a knot of a woman and uninviting to be around. Could teaching for almost three decades do that to a person? As time passed and teaching evolved Simmons seemed to stay mired in how things used to be. She helped many students win district and state musical awards but fell behind with the progression of new practices in education.

"Please enter Ms. Knight," responded Juice after my knock on his door. Entering he asked, "Would you like some French Vanilla Cappuccino?" Answering with much enthusiasm, "Yes, I would." Yummy, I thought. I love the smell of French Vanilla. There is excitement with the anticipation of the first sip. "We have a situation to address," Dr. J. states. In my head I asked the question, "Who did what now?" "Ms. Simmons has confiscated money from the school. She has been doing so for some time. The profit & loss spreadsheet that I asked you to look over contains evidence of this action," said Dr. J. It came to me that this was the storm. Now I am understanding why he asked me to look at the P & L sheet.

"Juice, from my eyes, the numbers seemed to balance," Juice continued, "Of course, on paper it looks great, but in my experience, I saw something that made me think differently. The numbers showed one thing, but the figures did not match up with the type of events. This is what we call doctoring the books. I made mistakes in the early years of my career trusting without verifying. I took for granted the word of an individual without checking their work. After my blunder, I learned what I missed. It happens. Learn from it and don't take it personally. I learned not to totally rely on someone else's words. You don't have to be leery of people, just follow what they say. Besides, in this position, the more relaxed you are, the more in tune you can be with your surroundings. Tenseness blocks intuition. Too much conscious concentration can cause one to overlook the obvious. Opening your mind is a developed skill. The revelation you seek is the obvious. I have learned to listen to a person's story and ponder on what was not said. I make sure that I verify the facts. People conveniently leave out pieces of information that benefits their cause." In wonderment I shook my head. Uninterrupted he continued, "To know the purpose behind a person's actions you must determine their intent. Finding this will strengthen your ability to make quality decisions."

Juice questioned, "Ms. Simmons conducted regular fundraisers with our students, right? "Yes, she did," I retort. "Each time she would take a small amount of the money and deposit it into her personal account. Sometimes she wouldn't do that. I figure she would make a purchase of a personal item and conveniently not document it. She could easily hide that transaction under a different category. Now think, she's had many years to perfect this and since there hasn't been a formal complaint, or someone in authority who has let her handle things without question. A check and balance system were never put in place, and because of that she has taken advantage of this opportunity." "She was stealing, but how?" I asked. Juice resumed, "She collected the money for each fundraiser, and before depositing she'd skim dollars off the top and submitted the remainder to the school's bookkeeper. It is easy to take a $100.00 dollar here and there from each event without it showing missing. Collect $2000.00 for a candy sale and not deposit two hundred. She covered her tracks by claiming there was lost or damaged product. Two Hundred Dollars is a nice chunk of cheddar. Do this once or twice a year for twenty years and you have collected, well you can do the math." "Juice, how did you find out?" I asked. "I've seen something like this before. I trust my intuition. There is something about her vibe that made me investigate. I wanted unyielding evidence before approaching her. I did research with the fundraising companies and the number of units submitted to Simmons. I cross-checked both amounts along with her deposits. Based on the evidence, I calculated the numbers which gave me the approximate amount raised. The problem as I stated earlier was that there was never a check and balance system at the school holding her accountable. After getting away with it for so long that money became a staple in her income diet. Be ready for this. I called her to my office."

Simmons, at times, left a negative vibe on me, like a dark cloud. She was not the kind of person that I rushed to talk to. There was a knock at Juice's door. Ms. Simmons entered with her head downward. Her eyes shifted sneakily back and forth over the top of her glasses at me and then Juice. I felt that storm cloud enter with her. Was I the only person who noticed this? She took her seat. Dr. J. started, "I know with the two of us in this meeting it can cause a person to wonder. Do you have any idea why you were called?" Juice loved to ask the person for their assumption regarding a matter before telling its purpose. It was a method he used to open the communication channel. Based on what they stated, it often gave him more material to ponder and investigate. Questioning has this atomic bomb power. Ms. Simmons said she did not have any idea why she was there, but I am sure she knew. Simmons's facial expression was like stone sitting there, "I'm really clueless as to why I was asked here." Her lips tightened. They reminded me of dark, wrinkled prunes. Stop it! I told my mind.

"I need for you to address a situation of some unreported funds regarding your fundraisers." Juice called out some dates and amounts. "Do you deny any of this?" Simmons did not respond. I noticed a developing scowl on her face. Facetiously there was her beautiful, inviting countenance we loved to see. "Ms. Simmons, I need for you to verbally answer the question." "No, I have not taken any money," she snappishly stated. As Juice has taught me, people will omit information when sharing; therefore, in their mind they do not consider it a lie. What is most important is the definition of what is being discussed. People define things differently based on their interpretation. "Please understand that your actions pertaining to this matter were inappropriate and unacceptable. We have investigated and concluded with sufficient evidence..." It was then that she started to refute his statements. Her true self came out from her beautiful façade.

I turned my attention to Dr. J. He did not respond to any of her statements. He wouldn't allow himself to be distracted by her emotional outbursts. Dr. J. continued, "The official charge against you is employee theft. We called this meeting not for your defense, but to officially inform you of the school board's termination of your services." Simmons interjected, "What do you mean by termination? I am not leaving my position. You must be crazy! You may intimidate the others, but you are messing with the wrong person Juice." Her voice elevated in volume. The real Simmons was among us. "Are you sure that you want to do this Juice Jordan? Do you realize how long I have been at this school? My reputation is solid, and the parents are in my support. We both know the media loves allegations." Was she baiting him for weakness? Juice never flinched. "Well Juice, are you sure you want to do this?" she sarcastically asked. Simmons's threat did not seem to frighten Juice. He continued stating the next step in this process. Experience has taught him to be thorough in these matters. Jordan always said that the proof of burden is not upon the person making the allegation, but the one in defense. There is nothing more embarrassing than to make an accusation without evidence, especially when it comes to this occupation. Juice was a player who came with his A-game. Non-evidence will lead you to the arena of litigation.

Amazingly, Dr. Jordan never asked Ms. Simmons to calm down, nor did he raise his voice. He kept his topic laser-focus. Typically, a meeting of this type produces a rise in emotions which can lead to superfluous words and actions. Juice's calmness helped the meeting flow as smooth as it could. He concluded with the instructions of what she needed to address with H.R.

The lasting image I had was the darkness of her eyes. The whites turned deep red, centered with solid black pupils. Possessed looking, at least that was how I viewed them. Juice called for Officer Flowers. Simmons's balled her fist. I thought she was about to blow like Krakatoa. She angrily stormed toward the door and forcefully slung it open, knocking a hole in the wall. Upon exiting, she almost knocked over a student who happened to be passing by. Her words were clear as she walked off in the distance, "That arrogant bast#*d. He doesn't know that he is f**#ing with the wrong woman!" Quickly, Flowers followed behind her. Juice called for Mrs. Bond, "Please send a paraprofessional to cover for Ms. Simmons's classes. Also, please find one of our preferred substitutes to cover the position as a long-term assignment until we find a quality replacement. Thanks." Leaning in toward me Juice whispered, "I don't think we've heard the last from Ms. Simmons."

Juice was right. A couple of days later he was informed that Ms. Simmons acquired the services of an attorney. She made the case that she was treated inappropriately and falsely accused without evidence. She demanded to be reinstated in her teaching position, along with a formal public apology. "The area superintendent requested a meeting with me," stated Dr. J. "Should we be concerned?" I asked. "There's nothing to worry about Ms. Knight. The area superintendent and I planned our defense before this meeting with Simmons. I knew she was nitroglycerin, which was why I approached this matter carefully. When working with people that are crooked in motive, you expect this. Just be thorough at your job. As with all things plan and expect the best."

My mind visited the idea if Ms. Simmons's intentions were to show the staff her arrogance for Juice's professional demise? If she were successful, it would undermine our vision and destroy our growth. Simmons wanted to show the world that Juice, an agent of change, was not a superhero. Her motives presented that she was not here for the good of the students. She was cancer, left untreated over the years. Additionally, Juice shared that after Ms. Simmons left our meeting, she made fast tracks over to the superintendent's office to file a grievance. One thing Simmons did right when she made a scene leaving the building was, she got the attention of the busybodies. I saw some inching their way toward each other, whispering as she stormed out. However, there is a difference of being aware for the good versus stirring up trouble.

A few days had passed since Dr. J. had his follow-up meeting with Ms. Simmons. In passing, I asked had he heard anything since. Juice shared, "The superintendent didn't overturn the original decision regarding Ms. Simmons. After meeting with the district's attorney, I was informed that the evidence collected was solid and her lawyer could not overturn our decision." The School Board backed Dr. J. with its decision not to reinstate her. Personally, I am not a fan of sitting in those types of meetings. You must learn how to manage those emotions, or it will consume you to a premature retirement. What made Simmons into the person she is today? I tuned back into Juice's words. "The school district's attorney met with Ms. Simmons and her attorney for the finalization of her process. Her attorney countered with a proposal for a lump sum settlement. She tried to place fear into the district with threats of media exposure regarding her case. Her threats were expected. The inexperienced probably would have fell into her demands. Picture for a moment a visible news camera truck and crew in front of the school. That kind of attraction stirs up negativity in the community. The School Board felt confident that the district could overcome any media attention. However, the district's attorney reminded her that there are two sides to a story and bringing media attention meant that she would have to publicly answer for her involvement."

"Facing the media can be daunting. Imagine the balance needed to walk the ship's plank without being tossed back-and-forth. Maybe something clicked in her to where she saw how limited her power was and it best to sign the resignation papers. Patience and humbleness are virtues you know. It seems in this age that being a bully is often rewarded, but it is not. There is a proverb that reads, *it is better to be patient than a warrior who takes a city*. As quickly as she stopped to share, Juice went his way. Besides, I had matters to attend.

In my estimation of the teachers, the masses were becoming believers. The word shared in the school on Juice was that they valued his stoic demeanor. I think the staff also witnessed that he was not backing down from any challenge. I viewed him as an artist with great unbroken focus. Dr. J. knew how to shut out distractions to obtain his vision. A great artist's creation justifies the means. Juice's mission was to produce the best working environment for those who chose to excel in this business, and he made it at every available opportunity. I categorized him as a superhero, but in his own right he fought for morality and justice through sacrifice of himself for the cultivation of fertile educational grounds for students. Servicing with pleasure is rare in this time. Dr. J. shared his belief that students were our future, and they deserved the best preparation by hiring the best qualified teachers and protecting their instructional periods from classroom distractions or disruptions was priority.

Juice was setting the stage for our young students to emerge and lead. Through discipline, our future leaders can achieve, but without it, lonely is their trek through the valley of the mountains. Our students had much to lose by not having sufficient skill set and fortitude to compete. Community and global jobs and businesses were advancing without us. Can our students effectively change the world? Better yet, I want them to lead the world. The foundation we are building at Bethune Middle must be deep and wide like the foundation of the One World Trade Center. Juice's philosophy is to never complain about something when you can do something about it.

I needed data to correlate culture improvement and academic growth in the school. The students are a great source of information. The counseling suite was the perfect place. Dr. Myles Archibald, one of our school counselors, created a program for the student body to express their thoughts. Dr. Archibald has been at Bethune for a decade, and he's done an amazing job at staying connected with our students. When I say his last name, I chortle. I call him Archie or A. He is okay with it. I can only guess what he had to endure from his peers in his earlier years. He holds a weekly session with six students selected from various grade levels. Dr. A. made it clear to me that the group is not a student government body. These students are in the trenches and a viable source of information for our student body. A meeting was scheduled so I decided to listen and observe. Myles was gracious enough to ask the group's permission for my sit in. They agreed.

As adults, we become so goal focused that we are oblivious to our current surroundings. In those moments, it can be magical when the proper attention is given. I paid attention to my surroundings while in transit to this meeting. The halls were clear. Student loitering has diminished. The floors were litter-free. It boggles my mind on how students can enter a clean area and leave it trashed. It reminds me of sitting in my house, enjoying my TV shows and out of nowhere a spider or bug appears on the wall. I had just previously looked at the wall and nothing was there, but then this creature magically appeared. It bothered me to see my classroom littered with paper or food on my floor. I never could understand why the student would toss trash on the floor when there is a trash can. It almost appears they do that as a rite of passage. Lecturing or punishing the class for one person's disrespect or laziness wasn't productive. It's unfair to the class. It took me some time to come to the realization that I should stop inconveniencing the mass because of the few. I refocused on the present. It is incredible how much change has occurred since the start of the year.

Archibald's group was comprised of sixth, seventh, and eighth grade males and females. He respected the kids by not publicizing their identity. It just worked better for their privacy. Their selection criteria included that each must maintain a minimum B average and no office referrals. Dr. Archibald introduced me to the group. "Thank you for allowing me to sit in on your discussion," I stated. I saw an upward curvature of a smile from a couple, while the others talked to each other in a quiet tone. Commencing the discussion Archibald asked, "Since the beginning of the school year, has the climate of the school improved for the students?" A tiny hand elevates in the air, "I think the environment is okay. I mean, it's better than it has been since I've been here, but there are still issues with students disrupting learning and bullying." Archibald retorts, "Please elaborate." "I have two classes where the teacher is teaching and a couple of students constantly yell out or make silly comments, especially when a student asks or answers a question." "How does the teacher handle the matter?" asks Myles. "The teacher tells the student to be quiet and not to be disrespectful of their classmates, but they don't. It becomes frustrating because the idiots won't let up."

An eighth-grade student chimes in on the discussion. It only takes one to share before the others join in. "Eighth graders that have attended Bethune since sixth grade have had two and a half years of anarchy and foolishness as my mom calls it. Some students do not like coming because there seems to be no consequence for misbehavior whether on the school's campus or the school bus. I have noticed some changes, but it still seems like there is a lot left to do. Some of the problem students have moved on but it makes us wonder if we'll ever see things completely turned around before we graduate," he commented. Dr. Archibald listened. He did not try to give advice on how or what to say. His position was to pose questions to keep the students expressing themselves. "How much more time do you think it will take to turn things around?" I ask. A student answers, "Really, I don't know if it can be done?" Dr. Archibald asks, "How are parents instrumental in this process?" A mouse voice answers, "The parents who care have transferred their child to a private school or to a different public school."

"Why do you think this is happening?" I ask. "Students of those parents who care are no longer here," stated Serenity. "One of my friends attended here. Marquita had experienced bullying issues. Her parents followed the school's protocols to get the matter resolved. According to Marquita, the administration tried to reassure the parents that the school had a "zero policy" when it comes to bullying. They claimed they would stop the matter, but they didn't. Marquita later told me the administration tried to make it sound as though there was no bullying taking place. Basically, they concluded there was not anything they could do. I never understood how those in authority could turn their head from something that was against the rules."

"Marquita reported it to her teacher, her counselor, and her grade-level principal. The only consequence the offender received was a good talking to. The incidences increased. Her physical safety was threatened. Emotionally, she couldn't take it anymore. Marquita cried a lot in private. She told me once that she felt alone in this cruel, unforgiving world even when she was around other kids. The hurtful part to me was that I knew emotionally she was in bad shape and there was nothing I could do."

"One morning on the bus, she snapped like a rubber band. I remember her screams sounded scary. Whenever anyone attempted to talk to her or touch her, she'd scream. The bus driver pulled over and called for a school official to meet the bus to escort her off. Marquita was a student that did not bother anyone and followed the rules. After so many complaints by her parents over the phone and meeting with the administration, seemingly getting nowhere, her parents withdrew her from the school," stated Serenity. Tristan, a seventh grader, chimed in, "I recall that event on the bus. Bananas! Marquita lost it, like she said. It was sad to see her like that. She minded her business and bothered nobody. By her reaction, there was no doubt on that day she had enough."

"She goes to counseling regularly. Marquita texts me from time to time that she is better, some days more than others, and truly happier that she no longer attends this school. I thought since her parents were supportive volunteers, they would have gotten better treatment regarding the matter, but I was wrong," she concluded. "I see," I respond. Serenity made a valid point. This is what can happen to the students who do what is asked but unsupported when needed. When engaged parents with expectations for their child and their school see non-academic or behavioral gains in their child, eventually grow tired of the excuses and false words. Standing in the shoes of the parents, I can understand how tiresome it is to hear a school official say their hands are tied when it comes to a discipline issue. Their child has a right to a quality education like any other student. An epiphany cloud hovered. It is my duty to help make things right for the kids who want to learn.

The students continued. I listened. Most of the members agreed that some teachers were not consistent at reprimanding students for misconduct. They felt those teachers perpetrated reproof of students when an administrator was present, but they did not say a word when the administrator was not. One student questioned the reason why the students who commit the infractions received more attention than those who didn't. I asked, "Do the teachers respond compassionately to a student when they're informed of misconduct or intimidation?" Most of the members gave me an eye answer. Their gesture took me back to when I was young. My mom used to look at me with her eyes as to say, "Are you sure you want to do this now?" Those eyes would straighten me out without the need for words. I got it. I looked at my watch. It was time for me to make my rounds. This time was well invested. There is much more we must do at Bethune Middle.

When giving feedback to others, what are some benefits of asking the person you are communicating to as to what they would like from you? For example, would they like feedback? For you to just listen? Or to give advice?

_____

_____

_____

_____

_____

_____

_____

_____

_____

_____

_____

_____

_____

_____

_____

_____

What is most important to you when receiving feedback on your performance from your supervisor?

_____

_____

_____

_____

_____

_____

_____

_____

_____

_____

_____

_____

_____

_____

_____

_____

_____

_____

_____

7

"You're making me angry. You wouldn't like me when I'm angry."
                                                        --Bruce Banner.

There are moments when the time seems to pass slowly, and on this day, time moved at a snail's pace. The end of school year is near. Juice and I regularly discussed how effective we were at meeting the school's mission. After bus dismissal was opportune to reflect on the day. With the students out of the building and quiet, meant my mind was calm and free from the daily dosage of noise pollution. Kids are chatterboxes with their own self-winding mechanism. I was thankful for my day, but the seemingly lengthy day had taken its toll on me.

I needed to relax, and basketball was my favorite season. The school's basketball team only permitted the seventh and eighth graders to participate. The sixth graders were allowed to play as an intramural league. The games were well-structured, which provided the right level of competition for this age group. Surprisingly, our sixth-grade games were competitive. The student body was very supportive in attendance.

I initiated a conversation with Dr. J., "I think we've made progress, don't you? However, I see areas of needed improvement. It feels great to share the positives and hide weaknesses, but I'm in a safe space with speaking on my weaknesses. In the beginning, I felt overwhelmed with failures. I feel differently now. I figured out how to channel any anxiety into a productive energy source." Pausing for a moment of reflection I continued, "Particularly, some teachers and students are stubbornly resistant to our new culture. They refuse to change regardless of how much support we offer. As administration we needed to figure out how to handle this. Would we take the passive position of warning students multiple times?" Juice comments, "It is interesting that you asked. Have you ever thought about how society's hierarchal systems are ruled by fear, not inspiration?" I questioned,

"Ruled by fear?" "Yes, by fear. You see the hierarchy threatens people with negative consequences when things are not completed as directed. Often administration threatens teachers with punitive documentation for not following directives. Teachers threaten students with a discipline referral for not following their directive. This is what I mean by ruling by fear or ruling with an "iron fist." I pondered for a moment. I wanted to add my keenness to this conversation to show my wisdom. "Look at life as the game of golf. The sand traps are there, but you do not focus on them. You just make yourself aware of where to avoid." Juice agreed.

"Ms. Knight, it's pleasing to hear you speak in this manner. The greatest reward a teacher can receive is when a student shows growth in their learning. A wise book states that one must decrease for the other to increase. *Iron sharpens iron*, right?" he asked. "Right," I reciprocated.

Dr. J. continued, "I've been informed, by some students, that some of our wonderful teachers aren't regularly visible in the hall during their class transitions." "I will take a look," I respond. "Also, students have shared that certain teacher aren't addressing student reported issues." When an inquiry process begins, it usually brings out additional issues. Not that I am looking for extra, but it happens.

I believe people, children and adults, function better when they are given choices. Juice and I talk about this regularly. How we approach a person determines what type of response I may have in return. I remember when one of my students was having an issue with another student. I attempted to address the matter to end quickly, but this student was not going to make this easy for me. I offered some positive words hoping she would redirect herself to her assignment. She was determined to have her meltdown. Finally, I gave her a choice of letting the issue go or have me make a phone call to her parent. I made sure to include that I would share some extra things I have experienced regarding her behavior. I know that was extra, but I wanted her choice to lead her to her assignment. As tough as the student pretended to be at that moment, she didn't want her business revealed to her parent. Sometimes it is wise to let things go and forget about it." I stated. Juice continued, "Excellent! Watch the different reactions from the teachers when they see you holding the accountable to your expectations. Be easy and unpretentious through the process. The teachers expect aggressiveness on your part. They are accustomed to this type of behavior and will underestimate your humble approach. Observe, and most important, listen," uttered Juice. "Dr. J. Thanks." He flashed his smile, and I flashed mine. I walked away.

Justin, a seventh grader, stopped me. He was consistent with his daily salutations. As always, he greeted me on his way to class. However, I noticed something odd about his demeanor. Typically, he had a happy spirit about himself, but on this day it wasn't apparent. He walked by with a blank stare in his eyes and no smile. Justin hesitated for a moment as though he wanted to say more but did not. I stopped him and quietly asked him to come to my office after the start of class. I did not want the other students to know his business. They say assumption is truth when a person believes what he sees, and for him that is his truth. It is silly the things that we think about are sometimes outlandish. The students didn't need to see him walking with me. They make things that are often untrue like he going to snitch. Just maybe, he is about to be suspended. The point is that it doesn't matter the real reason, it sounds good to create a reason and spread it around.

Fifteen minutes later, Justin knocked on my door. His walk was slow, almost apprehensive as he entered. His countenance was blank and lifeless. "Please, come in and take a seat. Thank you for coming. I want you to feel comfortable to share what is weighing on your mind. I know it can be easy to keep things contained but if you don't talk about your issue the stress of it can cause an unhealthy buildup. Many of our illnesses stem from unresolved emotional issues. When I passed you earlier, your eyes seemed to communicate something to me that I have not seen before. Is there anything you would like to share?"

Justin opened his mouth as to speak then paused. Whatever was happening, his action made me think it was something major. A person never knows what another is experiencing in life. Our busy life causes us to overlook other's humanity. This hustle-paced life has killed our compassion for each other. At that moment, I was not going to let that happen to Justin. In a low tone he stated, "I...I've been going through some things at home. My parents are not getting along, and I am afraid they may divorce. They do not talk to each other as loving people should. They argue in the morning and evening even when I am around. My home is not happy. When I am at school my focus in class is not there. Most of the time, I am on another planet. The crazy thing is that I do not remember anything from the previous day. Some days are better than others, but this thing they are going through is messing with my head. I have always lived with both of my parents. What will I do if they divorce?"

He paused, then continued. I saw anxiety in his face. "Lamont and James along with Stacy are bullying me. I'm frustrated." "When you say bullying, please describe what has happened," I stated. "The boys mostly talk. Most of the abuse comes from them in class and transitions. Occasionally, Lamont and James have put their hands on me. It typically happens when they know a teacher is not close. They have taken my work and hid it. When they are really feeling good, they tear up my work in front of me and throw it in the trash. Sometimes, when I go to the restroom during class change, the boys sneak in and jack me up. They run when they hear someone coming."

"What have you done in response?" I asked. "I've told teachers about my issue but soon learned that it was a waste of my words. I was taught that telling someone when invades your space after being told to stop was the right thing to do. I'm not the only one with this issue. Other students have reported their incidents of being bullied but they stopped when the person in authority didn't act on it. The person in authority just made light of what happened. Do you know how humiliating this is? I wanted to believe that a teacher would take a stand, but after so many times of telling with no results, I just learned to keep my mouth shut. Apparently, the bullies are above the law. But no worries, right? I get it. I keep my hurt inside." said Justin. "Have you told your parents about what's going on with you?" "No, I haven't. They are dealing with their own issues, and at this point, I do not want to trouble them."

I took a moment to process what Justin told me. I could see the hurt in his face and hear the pain in his voice. I felt like I needed to come through for this kid. I didn't know how close he was to the door of depression. Depression is a battle for an adult let alone for a child to navigate through. Being young is synonymous with fun. Children are full of energy and play. The weight of the world is not their responsibility.

We need more adults with caring, protective hearts who are willing to act. Students have the right to go to school in a safe space. I contemplated my childhood. My experience was different. My empathy meter increased for this kid. My travels as a child were not as cumbersome. Mom and dad kept open communication with me. Often, they checked in to see how I was doing, I mean how I was handling life as an adolescent. That is a crucial time for a young person. It is a period when a kid must figure out life and how does he fit in. The most important piece for him is to have access to a mentor. Many kids today do not have a wise mentor to talk to, and as a result, they are making some regrettable life decisions. Children should never be unhappy about life. I was at a moment when I felt I needed to say, "On behalf of the adults, I apologize for us not being there when you needed them." Apologizing was my first action and the second was to pursue the matter with the kids he mentioned.

I thanked Justin for coming and let him know that I am willing to help if he permitted me. He gave me a partial nod as to indicate a yes. I wrote him a pass back to class. He got up to leave. Before going out of the door, Justin looked back at me as if he wanted to say something, but he did not. I felt good that I was able to talk to him. I hoped that he knew that disclosing his feelings was a steppingstone to confidence and know that not all adults were not self-absorbed. I looked at the names again.

My attention focused on the parents of our students. Parents need to be in tune with their child's life. I recalled a conversation my parents and I discussed what they called a generation gap. When the age differences caused a difference in opinion regarding matters of life. Typically, there is a disconnect. Today, the generation gap seems wider than ever before with parents clueless of the activities in their kid's life. Children have been turned over to the authority of technology with unlimited access. They are unmonitored on the internet, video games, and smart phones. It is easy for children to get lost in their world if the adults are not diligent at staying connected. It is ironic that the devices created to entertain children, left uncheck, are now weapons of destruction. I started my calls to those parents of the accused, but I needed to check out a couple of things before I called. One of the worst things I could do was to call these parents without due diligence.

It is commonplace to see anti-bullying posters posted on the walls. At that moment, it disturbed me to think about them on our walls. Were they posted only as propaganda? Or are those in authority honoring the honorable students with support and corrective action toward those that break the rules?

My parents made it a habit to ask me about my low and high points of my day. Now that I am older, I understand the power behind this approach. This was their expectation so I knew I would be asked when I arrived home. By asking their child, a parent can gain insight on their child's activities, and asking drives better conversation. I know teenagers fight for their privacy, but I believe there is piece of them that want their parents to know what is going with them. There is a fine line here that can easily be crossed if not careful. Parents who want to know what their child is doing at school should volunteer their time at the school. The benefit of parents volunteering at the school is that it can influence the behavior of the child. Ultimately, it is a beautiful thing to see parents in the school. Their visibility is powerful.

A child that does not learn how to regulate his behavior eventually will have someone to regulate him. When it happens, he will not appreciate how they go about it. Disciplined comes with a loss of freedoms. I make it an emphasis to communicate to the student body to be proactive at deterring harassment and bullying. Staying consistent is the best method to get a point across. When a student commits an infraction, I apply the given consequence. I do not administer consequences based on my emotions. That is a definite mistake for me and the students. I feel better knowing that when I walk out of these doors for the evening, I sleep soundly at night. Unchecked emotions can get you in serious trouble. The accountability of student safety is both educators' and students' obligation. Parents trust us by sending their child to school safely and they expect him or her to return safely.

I called those three students to my office. Theatricality is a good quality to have when reprimanding, especially when you want to send a message to the bystanders. I purposely used the public announcement. I wanted the student-body to hear their names called. A cultural change was taking place, and I loved it!

Lamont, James, and Stacy entered with a perplexed look. I giggled inside; knowingly, they knew it was time to pay up for their actions. Do you have any idea why you were called to my office? I was fascinated listening to their reasons. I was taught at an early age to only answer what you have been asked. People tend to talk too much and share extra information when they are trying to hide something. Once the information is shared it becomes a conversational piece. After listening, I detected by Stacy's posture that she was the person who would give me what I wanted. What was important to me was how she tried to avoid answering my questions. The boy's facial reactions were priceless when she responded. They tried to discreetly coax her not to say anything. One of the boys gave an audible cough which was a warning to shut your mouth.

I decided to go in, "You're here because I have received an anonymous report that you three are bullying people (their eyes grew big like an owl's). Please understand, I'm not asking if you were bullying. You are facing a serious allegation and if it continues, you will be facing some serious consequences. Bullying is a very serious matter. Each of you have been in school long enough to know this. This administration is unswerving when it comes to the well-being of our students. In our eyes, bullying is non-negotiable. I am officially putting you on notice and documenting this conference. If I learn of another report about you three bullying, I will apply the maximum consequence. This behavior will expedite your transfer to another school. Do you understand?" They each nodded yes. I had Demont repeat back to me what he heard me say. He got it right. I observed Stacy. She had this bewildered look. I assessed that she was looking for a way out but did not have the courage to ask. I sent the boys back to class first. I kept Stacy to further our conversation. Sometimes a person needs a jump start to move forward. "Stacy, I kind of felt that you wanted to tell me more than you did but couldn't because of the Lamont and James." She gave a nod to say yes.

I wanted to peek at her reasoning for her association with the boys. I knew I wouldn't get an honest answer with the boys present. To my surprise she quickly jumped in with answering my questions. "Lamont, James and I became friends in the first grade. I guess our harassing others started then. I thought this is kid's stuff, right?" "How did you feel about that? Did you notice that your actions traumatized others?" I asked. After asking the questions I could tell that she was processing. She responded, "I don't know. I guess I saw...no I knew it was wrong for us to do what we were doing." "Have you ever had anyone bully you?" I asked. Stacy answered, "Yes." "How did it make you feel?" "It bothered me. Every day I had to face that person. Sometimes, others joined in on my horror while the bystanders watched. Occasionally, I thought I would hear a voice speak up in my defense, but that person was quickly silenced by the mass. I couldn't blame the voice who spoke up. It can be scary to have a mob of people yelling at you. Have you ever had that moment of humiliation when what it seemed like the world was watching? My hope for this nightmare to end ended as the days passed. I started to believe that being bullied would stay with me throughout school, until Lamont and James appeared. I never really asked why they brought me into their fold. It didn't matter because it was my opportunity to break free of my darkness. So, I did." "From the tone in your voice it sounded like it was a sad moment in your life. So, knowing how you felt, why do you think you did the same to other students?" "I guess...I don't know. I suppose I made myself believe that it was better to do it to others before they did it to me. I felt I owed something to them for helping me." I understood how she felt as I recalled my encounter of being bullied. I felt embarrassed and the associated pain was something I would never wish upon my enemies. It makes you wish you could disappear from society. I asked, "Isn't it terrible to be the target? Where did this influence start, neighborhood or school?" She looked perplexed with my last question. So, I added, "In some neighborhoods, life is about surviving, and this includes at school and home. Stacy responded, "No, that wasn't my life, but I did have to deal with the verbal harassment. If I didn't have a comeback I would become the target."

I found myself listening intently. Part of me wanted to judge and offer advice, but I do not think that it would have been accepted. I wanted her to have a listening ear from an adult who wouldn't tell her about the right and wrongs of life. I believe she already knew the difference between right and wrong, even though she committed wrongdoing. I replied, "I understand. No one likes to be picked on. Some believe that it makes you tougher, but it can make you angry and mean. I learned I had a choice to fight or run. Fighting back, motivated by revenge, makes a person hurt others, even those who deserve it. This type of person tends to lash out at anyone in their path. Essentially, their life is taken over by their behavior. Their own self-image is damaged. Do my words make sense? I want you to know that you have potential. You can offer the world your goodness. However, you can't show the world those good things if you continue hurting others." I paused, hoping this message was being digested. I asked, "Stacy, have you ever thought about finding new friends? Have you heard of the phrase that birds of a feather flock together? Perhaps you should take some time to think about which flock you're interested in being." I concluded our conversation. Stacy returned to class. Before walking out, I asked, "Who do you want to be?"

I made my call to Lamont's and James's parents regarding their allegation and explained the school's position. I made sure to convey that this administration will follow through with the appropriate consequence.

I turned my thoughts to the importance of our school culture. The lifestyle in some neighborhoods is the dog-eat-dog life. The weak are separated by the predators for their use. Compassionate people hate to see this act of nature, but this compassion doesn't stop evolution. It becomes the responsibility of a person to learn how not to become a member of the weak. The dog-eat-dog world lives by this code of fighting for their reputation and respect equates to their ticket of success.

Surviving this battle can be emotionally unhealthy. In this age, kids are suffering from emotional distress. Unresolved issues mean kids growing up to be adults with emotional issues. The result is a continuous unhealthy cycle. The popular known statement of *sticks and stones may break my bones, but words will never hurt* are inaccurate. Hateful words cause emotional wounds in the young and carried over in the adults. What is their recourse? One must learn to develop thick skin.

I work to keep this issue logically in my head. There is a difference between aggressive and assertive. Aggression doesn't consider the well-being of the person. I believe what we see in the behavior of kids comes from aggression. People who live in this world with low self-esteem are constantly having to cope for survival. I take a stance on advocating for the unvalued.

The boys' parents gave their excuses to condone their child's behavior. It was pathetic to hear. I understand why Lamont and James act the way they do. I deflected what each parent had to say. I couldn't afford to take in their nonsense. I stayed firm with my call. The worst thing I could do was to show any weakness in my position. Being weak hurts our students who are complicit with our rules. Both knew that I was consistent with following our rules. I understand that a policy is a guideline to follow, not the end all or be all. Yes, we are human and depending on the given situation, some leniency should be considered. I had a moment of thinking on a grand scale. What if all people chose to live by principles and not their selfish desire? Communities may change for the better, won't they? I smiled at that. However, when authority doesn't act, they enable the unjust to become our menace. I consider three types of people in this world, the docile, the daring, and the law breakers, who are the kids that love to push the boundaries.

Springtime was present and this meant standardized testing. Schools are about testing and data. This was also March Madness. It is the time when college basketball teams come together for tournament play. The nation's fans watch excitedly and angrily who wins. The collegiate analysts survive off coffee and no sleep. Comparing the two, both experience a testing of who can win in this March madness. As the testing coordinator, my responsibility is major. My worry level is high. One error can cost me my job. There is much effort given to adequately prepare the teachers for an ethical win. Standardized testing is the data the school systems use to measure student growth. So, any testing mishap can publicly taint a school's reputation. The Atlanta Public Schools incident caused a chain of events that impacted the way testing is administered. Some teachers and administration were caught cheating on their students test scores. Thirty-five of their employees were indicted for their involvement. Apparently, this group of educators organized a plan to enhance their student scores with intent of increasing their money bonuses. The personnel indicted included the superintendent, some test coordinators, principals, and teachers. Some of the accused decided not to fight their defense and accepted a plea-bargaining deal for decreased prison time. In the end, eleven were convicted of Racketeering. The tradeoff for the money versus prison time would have been a no brainer for me. I believe in the rules, and I believe in consequences, but some consequences should deter an individual. The media served this incident on a platter for months to the public. The people involved must have been told not to tell their side of the story, but maybe their story deserved to be told. It really made me wonder if the teachers were the mastermind behind this or was it the higher echelon? I was dumbfounded to know that a teacher could go to prison for that level of crime, but naïve I was not to the fact that their teaching certification would be revoked. Was the justice system using this as an example?

Jordan did not base our success on the yearly standardized test. He used data, but standardized data was not the premier indicator. He made his philosophy clear on this and not the politically correct version. Juice understood that student scores would automatically increase by eliminating classroom disruptions and adding a positive school culture. According to his statements, these two elements equated academic success.

At my former school the staff was programmed for standardized testing. Standardized testing drove our focus in our Professional Learning Community meetings. The closer Spring approached the crazier things became. It was an unhappy time of the school year for me. I believe all teachers were on edge and with that kind of pressure, it caused all to stress more than we should have. Your performance can suffer because of it. High stress can cause some to doubt their capabilities, and when doubt appears, normal decisions become questionable. What was really depressing for me was that maintaining my position depended on my students test performance. They needed to show the gains from the previous year.

The stress level for a teacher is high. It starts from the time you enter the building until you exit. The experience of being a teacher assists with my teachers. I have the empathy to know what being overwhelmed looks and feels like. I shared my thoughts with Dr. J. for his wisdom and approval. I told him how I read an informational piece that stated how people in business and life could perform better if they learned to manage energy, not time. So, I thought about how this could apply to educators? Teachers could lower their stress by managing energy, not time. The writing explained that managing time is ineffective if the person runs out of energy. People who revitalized themselves periodically throughout the day were able to maximize their workday and not deplete themselves of energy. Think about the profession of law enforcement. Most would probably agree that law enforcement is a high-stressed occupation, but I feel that education is equally stressful. Teacher burnout is regular, and because of the bureaucracy, new entry teachers tend to change professions within their first three years. Some have expressed that there is too much to deal with uncooperative parents and students. One aspect to consider is that all teachers should be supported by its administration. One of my dad's quotes stays with me. It is better to be celebrated, not tolerated.

Somewhere, in this focus of standardized testing, the real essence of it has become misdirected and distorted. Will our educational system change its direction. Another point to think about is after testing. Our students believe that class work after testing is done for the year. There are approximately three weeks of school remaining. The teachers and administrators begged, threatened, and everything in between to have the students apply effort to their class assignments. It didn't work. The school environment was bananas. I felt I had better success with spreading thick, cold peanut butter on a slice of bread than changing the mindset of my students. How this practice developed is unbeknownst to me. Combating this issue became too much for some teachers. Some teachers went with the flow that academic teaching was done. They would print off worksheet packets or lead them to do workbook assignments. The end of the year became three weeks of turmoil. I didn't want to be the person who complained so I offered possible ideas to help change things. However, I learned to keep my ideas to myself. As much as I thought I was constructively helping by offering ideas for improvement, I ended up having a target placed on my back.

School is not over until the last calendar day. I wished the School Board would change the district calendar for our testing dates. My idea would be to move the testing dates to the last two weeks of school. Since the test is administered over a two-week period, the last completion date day would be on the last day of school. The teachers and students would not have to be subjected to the uncooperative mindset of the students. My guess is that schools would have most students present to do testing with less behavior distractions. The test results could be electronically submitted to the schools. The parents could acquire an access code to see their child's scores. The hard copy results could be mailed over the summer. My idea may not have been the best, but I thought it could be a seed.

Based on our current school culture for our students and teachers, I believe Juice and I have effectively transformed this school into a positive environment. Our students are expected to uphold a high standard. Our culture allows our teachers the ability to teach and the students the environment to learn. Student discipline starts from within, not from the teachers forcing. Forcing someone to do something they don't want to do is a waste of energy. I started in a system where the students were coerced to do their academic work which squandered my energy. It was defeating for me to leave the building drained while the students walked out with full energy. By their actions, I swear they had been drinking energy drinks throughout the day. Bethune's motto is *By Choice, Learning Comes First.* It is spot on, and I love it. We are not in the practice of creating robots. That is what happens when children are forced to learn when they clearly show they do not care. I think it was evident that the rebellious could not thrive here.

Regarding the topic of self-discipline, our staff is expected to operate with high standards. Mrs. Derryberry's name popped into my mind. She spoke with disdain toward the students. Her voice was gruff and mean. The students openly express how they did not like her. I could dig it. The way she speaks to them rubs me the wrong way. She tenured with thirty years behind her in the school district. You can say she is a dinosaur. Teachers who have been around for a long time sometimes believe that they are entitled in their position. Typically, they are set in their traditional ways; sometimes unwilling to adopt new practices. Some are bold enough to believe they cannot be released from their job. Today, things are different. What was allowed then isn't permitted now. Derryberry has worn out her welcome at Bethune. The students need to be respected. There are times when their behavior can grate on your nerves, but they are kids. Kids will play at the wrong time then turn around and surprise you with good behavior when you least expect it. Most times they do not perform when you want them to. Even kids will put up with so much meanness from an adult.

Mrs. Derryberry joined our staff after the first month of the school year. She filled the position of Antonio Alverez who did not work out. He was lazy and did not meet his deadlines. The School Board terminated him rather quickly. Some students were interviewed during his due process. It was revealed that he never engaged in any conversation with the students while glued to his computer. His classes were assigned worksheets for their work. Of course, the students took advantage of that situation. They plugged into their music, ate snacks while posting selfies on Instagram or Snap Chat. Their investigation revealed that he was searching the internet for jobs. It was totally unfair to his students. Human Resources filled his position with Derryberry. Apparently, they thought she was the "appropriate fit." I guess the appropriate fit meant she was state certified, mean, and experienced. I believed H.R. knew what they were sending to this populace. My mind rambled. I needed to work on that.

Thinking about Mr. Alverez, one of the unknown aspects in hiring is that the candidate may seem like the right fit, but you do not know what you are getting until they come onboard. I call it the Cracker Jacks syndrome. As a kid, I would eat my Cracker Jacks loaded with caramel popcorn with a passion just to reach the prize at the bottom. The occasional issue I found was the prize may have been one that I didn't want. Those moments were not exciting. In the beginning, I understood Derryberry's rough approach, but now I see that it was not an act to get the students acclimated to structure. It was her normal behavior. The students spited her with annoyance. Middle school behavior can be immature and irritating. Her voice was loud, and it carried throughout the hallway.

She wasn't the right fit, but even with her disdainful nature, Dr. J. did not want to transfer her during the school year. Even under her negative leadership, Derryberry equated stability. Her leaving in mid-year meant introducing a new variable which could cause her students to academically fall behind and that was something Juice did not want to consent. Students depend on consistency, even if it is negative. They may not like the person, but it is reassuring to have their presence daily. For the students' sake, he kept her. However, Derryberry had pushed past the boundary of acceptance.

Dr. Juice was done. He had enough of the complaints from the students and their parents. It was time for Mrs. Derryberry to do her good elsewhere. I totally got it. Her name humored me when I said it. Dr. J. included me in her exit conference.

Juice prepared me before her conference. He had received transfer approval from H.R. Although I knew it was best for Mrs. Derryberry and the students, I had mixed feelings sitting in front of her while Juice explains her reason for her transfer. Some of the teachers have overtly expressed they did not like Jordan, and I believe that Mrs. Derryberry was one of them. I never heard her express it in words, but I could see it in her actions. I listen to a person's words, but I pay closer attention to their actions. A person's body gestures communicate a lot. Their attitude exudes itself in their action.

Words are spoken but fickle actions do not lie. Jordan has stated that the same people who praise you, can crucify you. Valuing another's opinion of you is valueless. People change like the shifting of the wind and if you are not emotionally sound, it can be a hurtful blow when it happens. My expectation is what I need to live up to. I keep in mind my norms I follow are to respect myself, respect others, and respect the school.

Besides, there are boundaries between work and personal relationships with your colleagues. It made sense to me when I heard a pastor refer to relationships as spatial. A person's life is represented as the core and the people they associate with have a spatial placement in their life. The people that are close to the person in the relationship are located near the inner circle or the center. People that are not close to you with their relations are located further away from you, your nucleus. Typically, the inner circle is made up of family and close friends. However, that is not always the case. Depending on how you feel about a certain family member, he or she may not be in your inner circle. Simply, the closer in proximity the more intimate you are with them.

Considering this concept, I clearly saw how my colleagues were spatially located in my circles. What is interesting to me is how great work can be accomplished even when your relationships are not close in nature. Getting the job done was not about being a family or friends, but through respect, systems, and application. Organs in the human body are a perfect example. The bible speaks on the body having members within and their functions. Each organ is unconcerned with worrying which organ is in charge. Each operates by its purpose. The heart is not interested in controlling the brain and the kidneys are not looking to lead the liver. Concerning work, I did not need to share my private life with my colleagues for us to get things done. This spatial concept represents intimacy and distance. Understanding this principle keeps the mission the main thing and colleagues productive.

Derryberry made it to Juice's office. He started the meeting with the reminder of the school's mission. It took me a second to figure out why he used this approach. Shortly, my answer came. The school's number one goal is the betterment of our students and by doing so, he made clear the central topic of the meeting. Regardless of her response, the mission is the goal, and her actions were not leading the students to our goal. I figured she would argue with him, but she didn't. Maybe

Derryberry was ready to move on to a different environment.

Juice gave her the name of the new school she would be transferring to along with her new teaching assignment. She asked a couple of questions. Juice answered them as best he could. If a person does not ask, they won't know. I think Dr. J. worked with Mrs. Derryberry as best as he could. There were times when he would overlook some incidents. I think she took advantage of this kindness. Over time, her actions descended further to the dark side. The H.R. department backed his decision for her transfer. I must say that he has clout to have his decision approved before the end of this school year.

Some leaders are efficient at not offering support to their staff. Let us call it "hands off leadership." I understand the concept that all people need to be told daily how wonderful a job they're doing. However, even the strong people appreciate hearing periodically that they are valued. Acknowledgement is major. Even the smallest gesture of appreciation is welcomed, and it does wonders. The hands-off approach and letting things happen without guidance and feedback can be negligent.

After our meeting with Mrs. Derryberry, I wanted to meet with Jordan and talk about next year's plan. We confirmed an afternoon for our appointment to discuss next year's layout. A passing thought entered my mind on how quickly our first year at Bethune has passed. I smiled as I thought about the end of the school year when there would be no students. In my mind, I was doing my happy dance. Metaphorically, our air quality is healthier than at the start of the year. The teachers are more cordial and appear to like being at work. I have seen more jovial smiles these days.

Dr. J. and I met as coordinated. I took note of his board when I entered his office. It was filled with diagrams and notes. He used one of my favorite organizers, the web format. Webbing has a revealing connection. This was a special moment for me as I was privy to see the planning process behind this champion.

A champion, I pondered…I remembered a scene from a movie that I love. Two friends were conversing about life. One tells the other that he lives life at a high altitude. He compares his life to flying at an altitude of 36,000 feet and sometimes higher. He said the average person doesn't aspire much from life and is okay with flying at 10, 000 feet. They accepted being average and flying at low levels with most. This is the average group who doesn't expect much from life. He chooses to soar at a higher level because he demands more from life. The advantage of the air space at higher heights denotes less traffic with a clearer view below. I resumed my study of the board. Juice observed me looking at his notes. "Take a minute to digest Ms. Knight," he says. I read his essential question. I chortled, not at the question, but his application of the question on the board. It is difficult to release the teacher. The power of the EQ sets the focus for the learner. It is an initiator for critical thinking, or even better, it is the why. The question was simple. What does success look like for our stakeholders at the middle school, high school, and globally?

Dr. J. took me on a tour of his color-coded webbing. "As you can see, I have a list of the faculty and staff for next year. Next to their name I have included the content areas they are qualified to teach, and grade level. One of the selections is currently working at another school. It is okay. I have already received confirmation that he is able to join our team. I like to compare us as a performance-based company. I seek performers that have shown a history of quality performance. Early in my career, I decided that I did not want to totally rely on others to bring me some winning personnel. Therefore, I spend a fair amount of time scouting and recruiting for the right people. To be honest with you, my system has been successful. I won't lie to you and make think that I have selected all winners. Occasionally, I have had some busts, but very, very few. It would be nice to never make a mistake, but that is impossible. I've learned from my mistakes which helped me to decrease them in the future."

"That's interesting," I stated. "Do you always get your person?" "No. Sometimes the timing may not be right, or I am not in the best position to offer the principal of the person what they need in exchange. To make it work the releasing principal must feel rewarded. I pride myself on giving the other organization equal or better value of what I'm receiving." "So, are you saying that this process is more about giving than receiving?" I ask. "Yes, you're correct. Look at the big picture. The more I am proactive helping others get what they want, the better positioned I am at getting what I want. It's a win-win." "Juice, the way I see you working this is like being the manager of operations for a professional sports team orchestrating a deal." We both smiled.

"I am creatively thinking who my ally can be. Sometimes I look outside of the educational field for teachers," Juice shares. "Are you saying that you have no problem recruiting outside of the education field?" "No, I don't. You see I have found that a key to successful teaching is understanding people to inspire them. This person is adept at creating pictures for students' minds. For example, my success comes through empowering educators that know how to facilitate a strong self-image within our students. Behavioral psychologists' research indicates that a person's self-image determines what we can do in life. A person's aspirations will never rise above his level of how he views himself. If his esteem is low, his accomplishments will meet those levels. I select teachers that are effective at influencing others, and when I say influence, I mean relational leading. I cannot tell you the countless number of teachers who state they are in the business of helping students when truthfully, they are there for their own benefit. School becomes their means to an end. Be leery when you hear "I've done this, I've done that, or without me it wouldn't have" indicates selfish intent. I look for teachers who know how to encourage young students to tap into their potential with the expectation of nothing less than their best. For me it is not about this "tough love" approach. It is amazing to me to see how futile it is to force a student to do something for their own good. Really, how can another person really know what is good for that person? Now that I have expressed my previous comment, regardless, as teachers we cannot afford to sacrifice structure, order, and expectations for those who choose minimalism and mediocrity."

"I understand!" Juice continued, "Now, going back to my focus on why I selected someone who's not an educator. Teaching teacher skills is easy. Any person can plug into a system, but the person I select must have a confident self-image and evidence of successful productivity. He needs to be inspiratory, able to breathe new life. This guy was not a certified teacher, but I made sure he received support to guide him through the certification process. He and I commenced talks for this opportunity a few years prior. He stuck with it and became certified. This approach was a gamble. He could have changed his mind at the last minute and not gone through with this. My time and resources would have been for naught. I made sure I kept the lines of communications open. I figured the more he felt that I was honest about things, it would assure him that he was valuable to this program. The key to this plan is that the teachers you see have shown that they are rooted and grounded in our system."

Juice continued, "The problems I see in schools aren't antiquated buildings or lack of technology. The cause for the decline in our schools relates to poor parenting, lazy teachers, and administrators who are not bold enough to take back their position of authority. The issue is created by adults and the resolution lies with them. The greatest impact of change starts with the parents. A parent is the first educator their child encounters. It is their responsibility to foster a culture of structure, favorable environment, and positive encouragement."

"It's a shame to hear a parent say that they don't know what to do with their unruly child." The word "unruly" resonated in my mind. It is a powerful descriptive. Listening to him, I thought about how instrumental a parent is at fashioning a young life. I understood what he meant about parents who confirmed they could not control their child. I have heard it from some of my students' parents. How can an adult allow a child to rule their environment? I figured out that it is the parent's behaviors that allow their child to become a societal monster. Did these parents suffer from low self-esteem? Or is it because some are so busy earning an income that they have misused productive time with their child. Children watch everything adults do. At this school, we are their model of what can be. Kids will take what they see and become better at it. That is not a bad thing unless the child is using it for the wrong reason. You know the saying "the apple doesn't fall far from the tree" is true. How would life be if more parents had a healthy perspective on parenthood?

As Juice talked, my mind swirled with thoughts. It is a waste to see a parent hold onto old, negative school memories. Those unresolved issues can rear its ugly head when their child experiences an issue at school. I have sympathy for them, but that person must release the past. Their past can form their future and their future leads back to their past. Battling backwards blocks battling forward. I don't mean to make light of a person's experience. Learn from it and keep things moving. I understand their issue, but my commitment is our school's mission, and I will not jeopardize the mission.

My confidence as an administrator is increasing. Acting helps overcome my fears. Action builds my confidence and confidence reciprocates more action. I am thankful that Juice brought me on the team. Excited and nervousness blinded me, but he knew what he was doing, right? There are times when I think he has x-ray vision. It is like he can see through you. He sees your potential, even when you are unaware. The secret of achievement is what one thinks and believes they can do. Talent helps, but the power of belief is explosive.

"When will we disseminate next year's contracts to the teachers?" I ask. "They will be issued this week," responds Dr. J. I looked at my watch. Time passes quickly. I had duties to handle. Before I exited Jordan asks, "Do you have an answer to the essential question?" I answer, "Obviously, the teachers are the instrumental piece for our success. They are what make a school great. Teachers with a positive self-image and a strong belief in the school's mission do wonders for students. Having teachers with the right attitude is like the artist constructing a masterpiece." My mouth pauses but my thoughts continue. "Great teachers devour training to be the best. One must acquire the best training and plenty of it. I feel we are as strong as our weakest teacher." Juice responds to my answer, "Success only has a chance when you have the right people. Right people are self-motivated. A leader does not consume time micromanaging them. A leader's energy is not spent getting their staff to do the job. Right teachers do their work and do it well." Jordan gives a smile of approval like a teacher gives his student when she gives an intellectual answer. "Do you have your plan on hard copy?" I ask. "Yes," he tells me. "May I have a copy?" "I will get Mrs. Bond to make it for you."

I reflected as I went to my office. I thought about what I can do to contribute to our school to strengthen it. I am compelled to carry my weight here. I could open a communication channel for collaboration between the teachers and the students. It would provide a platform for them to share ideas. Yes, that is what I will do.

I think a great leader knows his craft. Like a parent who supports their child to become greater than themselves, so does a leader do for his team. I believe people respond better when they have sufficient information. Better decisions can be made when you have sufficient information. I am not naïve. I know there are two sides to a coin. The other side, depending on your circumstance, can be better left unsaid, but I believe a staff that is knowledgeable can produce more than one that is left unaware. A clueless staff will fill its mind with its own thoughts and conclusions and those conclusions can attack the fabric of our success. Their action becomes an infectious disease that takes over and destroys the smallest inkling of hope.

I creatively brainstormed how I could increase my efforts at connecting with the students, teachers, and the community. My success depends on my relationships with the people. The better connected I am the more I can ask people for their help. When a person believes he is valued, you can ask that person to run through a brick wall. People need to know that I can be trusted. As a teacher, I hated the disloyal leader. The law of reciprocity is real. When you value your people, they will value you. The term praise came to mind. I needed to praise the staff more. Genuine praise is powerful because it opens a door for connection. I knew how I felt when I received it. I am a person who does not need constant praise, but a dose here and there matters. You can be like a hard-shelled M&M candy, but within the interior lays a center of chocolate waiting to be melted. There is a book named *Acres of Diamonds* that compares the value of people to diamonds. Diamonds are a valuable gem and having them in your possession can make you rich. As crazy as it may sound, sometimes we can overlook a diamond right in their presence. I thought about how outside consultants are paid to come, observe, and recommend change. Consultants can cost a hefty price. I wonder if the principals ever considered the idea of using their own staff as consultants. Most organizations have qualified individuals that can assess and recommend.

During my moment of reflection, I felt this surge of energy. It was like an athlete getting their second wind. I had a sense of power and true purpose. As I walked the campus, I took the time to genuinely converse with our students. I asked them about their thoughts on our school. I wanted to know how their day was and how things were going in class. Next, I went to the teachers. I wanted to see if I could do the same with them. If their suggestion were something I could immediately put into effect, I made it happen. I wanted my actions to speak for me. People become believers when they see your actions.

Dr. J. caught me later in the day. He informed me that we were taking a field trip. Hmmm, I thought. Did he mean for me to be present or plan the fieldtrip? I guess my face showed perplexity as Juice stated, "I meant for you and me to go on a fieldtrip." "Sure," I replied. My curiosity was amped on where he planned for us to go. Juice continued, "We're going to observe a gentleman named Tanner Midnight. He is the recruit I mentioned in the plans for next year who has agreed to join our team." I felt my excitement rise. This is the first time I have experienced something like this. As a teacher, I did not go on many field trips with my students. I wanted to but my students' behavior was not suited for a fieldtrip. Their disrespectful behavior was too much within the school, let alone out in the public. I didn't have the parental support, or the backing needed from the administration when it involved misconduct.

Teachers who understand the power of a field trip know that important learning takes place that you won't receive in the classroom. The classroom is useful, but it does not offer a real-life connection. Juice has approved three fieldtrips per grade level. Jordan believes they are a requirement. How else were the students going to globally compete if they were not exposed to societal environments? A school benefits from the financial support of businesses and partnerships.

Dr. J. shared more, "On our field trip, we are visiting a Fortune 100 corporation. The supervisor of Mr. Midnight approved our visit. When we are there, I want you to take notes on how he interacts with his colleagues. We will stay for a couple of hours and grab some lunch before returning to school." I thought about how the days at this time of the year are beautiful with plenty of sunshine and make for a refreshing car ride. It is satisfying to get out of the building and breathe in fresh air.

Juice and I stopped at the Vortex for lunch. I grabbed me a patty melt burger with some sweet potato fries. I passed on the soda for water with lemon. My selection was not the healthiest meal, but it was okay to splurge this one time. The environment was upbeat. Our food came out in a descent time frame. Apparently, we had placed our order before the lunch crowd. We ate and returned to school.

Upon our return, Juice and I traded notes about our fieldtrip. I shared, "Based on Mr. Midnight's interactions with his colleagues, he appeared to be understanding and cooperative. Specifically, there was some miscommunication on a project, but he seemed to keep his poise when some showed agitation. Blaming and arguing could have easily become the focus, but Mr. Midnight did not respond to it. He creatively applied alternative methods to correct things. I think because he did not succumb to blame his colleagues did not offer resistance. Maybe, it was because they were familiar with the way he does things. Whatever, I sensed respect in their relationships. What I liked most about Mr. Midnight was that he listened to his colleagues without interrupting. When a person shared their opinion, he listened. I think he is a person who is goal-focused and a team player." Dr. J. asked, "Based on our limited time, do you see him strengthening our staff?" "Before I can confidently answer, he and I would need to converse. I would want to know more about him. From what I saw, he could strengthen us with his leadership skills. I liked his humbleness. Yet, he showed a confidence about himself. If I really had my way, I would choose to bring him on board in a student-teacher capacity or an intern. Then I could watch him interact with our students in real time, but based on what I saw, I think he can fit into our scheme of things." Jordan nodded his head. I paused, waiting for Juice to add to my comment. He didn't. Welp, I looked at my watch as we made our arrival back at the school. I suppose I talked longer than I had anticipated. In this universe time is a currency and I must spend it wisely. As we headed to the school entrance, I let him know how much I appreciated our field trip. "I had a super-fantastic day!" I stated while yawning. Tonight, I thought, I am sure to sleep soundly. Tomorrow is a new day; one day closer to our goal.

Things were running smoothly when contract day arrived. Jordan sent out an email reminder to the teachers to sign their contract. It needed to be done within seven business days. Dr. J. schooled me on how it was back-in-the-day regarding contracts. "The district placed the responsibility on the principal to hand out the contracts. The teachers who signed their letter of intent were offered a contract. The awkward moment to this process was that it exposed the teacher who was not asked to return in the presence of the other teachers. I guess you could say that everybody knew your business. Additionally, there was the element where a teacher could become emotional about an issue in the contract they didn't agree to." When Juice broke down the intricacies, I got it. "This process really put the responsibility on the principal. I dealt with irate individuals. There was no rational answer to calm them at that moment. The best you can offer to the that person is to ask for their patience and understanding. For them, it was a moment to defend their position. Their income was their source of livelihood, and it was being severed. That can make anyone go ballistic. Being calm and not accusatory is a critical skill for us to have in our repertoire. The calmer you are, the calmer you can possibly help the other to be." He added that this method was not a 100% fool-proof, but it worked majority of the time for him. "Comparing the two, this new process is more confidential and so much better for all involved," he concluded.

The systems we put in place have made a difference. Measurable progress and quality teachers returning is what makes a school great. The teachers who were not a good fit in our system have been assisted to another environment outside of Bethune. I thought about our teachers and how do they feel about our changes. Would I hear comments about our noticeable change, gains or the contrary? Dr. J. was a person that planned. For our post planning, he scheduled a one-day training session off campus for the entire staff. To me it seemed strange to have a group training course at the end of the school year, especially with those who were not returning. Juice catered food for the staff to eat. I contemplated how interesting this event would be. You know human nature feeds a negative ego. Would those who were not returning cause mayhem?

Something to think about: Many times, we feel the need to lecture or tell someone our opinion.

What is the advantage of asking vs telling to get across a point? Are you a person who asks more than tells? How can you change this?

_____

_____

_____

_____

_____

_____

_____

_____

_____

_____

_____

_____

_____

_____

_____

_____

_____

_____

_____

How often do you think about asking open-ended questions over closed-ended questions for understanding and clarity?

_____

_____

_____

_____

_____

_____

_____

_____

_____

_____

_____

_____

_____

_____

_____

_____

_____

_____

How poised are you when asking questions, even during a tense moment? What does this look like for you?

8

"What happens now determines what happens to the rest of the world."
                                              –T'Challa, Black Panther.

The end of the year arrived after an interesting journey. It reminded me of a twisty rollercoaster ride. The up, down, and around motion can cause motion sickness. Poise was my focus word of the year. The calmer I was the calmer it made others. This rollercoaster of life and work had its share of twists. There was no need for complaints. Just like being on the rollercoaster, I needed to strap in because life does what it pleases. All I can control is my response to the challenge. My reactions defined me, and my human emotions made each event interesting.

There is an excerpt I love to read from a young writer of the book *Laws of Thinking*. He wrote that as human beings, one of the laws of life is the Law of Becoming. Success is the end result when a person diligently works toward his aspiration. As he progresses in his journey, his achievement is not a measure of doing, but being. So, when a person says, "I am" he is stating that he is the very thing he says. "I am" solidifies the fiber of our being, the balance in our mind, body, and spirit. Every collective organ works in unison to manifest the desired goal. Therefore, when I said that *I am* a teacher, I was acknowledging to myself and the universe that I was the thing spoken. My essence made me think, look, and speak as a teacher. The universe delivers what we profess. It is interesting how every person is in control of their thoughts, actions, and destiny. However, some are not mindful of this and wander through their life blaming others for their unhappy and unproductive life and spreading their infectious nature to those nearby.

The end of the year workshop arrived. I was appreciative for the last days of school. The morning of the workshop was beautiful. The air was cool and fresh, and I loved taking deep breaths which replenished my energy. My thoughts focused on the people leaving this year. How would they conduct themselves in this workshop? Quickly, my thoughts returned back to the euphoric moment of this sunshine and the mild temperature. The moment was perfect for my brown Tom Ford Jennifer sunglasses. I love their look and fit. They came with a cost, but well worth the investment.

I made my tour around the room to greet everyone. I could sense some mild apprehension from those who were not returning. I get it. I still had respect for their attendance. Would they be open to what the workshop had to offer? A closed-minded person is a detriment to himself and those around him. I stayed positive and believed the few would not influence the many.

I reminisced back to when I was in the classroom when I faced a similar scenario. I had a few infamous students with misconduct issues that could easily disrupt a learning environment. I knew their behavior could trigger the entire class to join in. I strategized ahead of time to diffuse their behavior for the sake of the majority. It was more work on me but expending the energy to relocate them if they became uncooperative. Planning paid dividends. One of the three started in with his disruption. I immediately sent him to another classroom. Because I did, the remaining students decided they wanted to learn. Now, how will Dr. J. handle matters with the non-returnees?

Truth is that tomfoolery can come from children or adults. Just like the students, teachers watch to see how meetings are conducted. If the presenter isn't proactive, it only takes one rebellious soul to take over.

Looking over the agenda, I saw that our focus was on the topic of discrimination. This caught my attention. I knew the definition of the term, but how would it be applied in this workshop? Being a Black American and living in the United States meant being exposed to discrimination. I caught myself and got back on track with my purpose for walking around.

Juice opened the workshop with a warm welcome and gratuity to those attending. He talked about the benefits received with an open mind. "I know some of you, not by choice, aren't returning to Bethune.

Regardless, accept this workshop as an investment for wherever you go. Let this moment create ideas within for growth. Today, our focus embroils discrimination. Yes, this can be a sensitive subject. Discrimination as denoted in Merriam Webster dictionary is "to make a distinction in favor for or of against a person or thing on the basis of the group, class, or category to which the person belongs rather than according to actual merit." Based on this definition, how many of you think you are guilty of this? How many of you feel you have experienced it? Discrimination can bleed out of the barriers of race. It can involve gender against gender, height and different body types, looks, behavior, and so on."

"I believe discriminating thoughts can impede a teacher from optimum performance. It is so common that most people may not be aware that they are infected with it. They wear their discriminatory practices like clothing. It becomes their way of life. Discrimination skews one's perspective. Just as a house that has a fence around it to keep out people and things, so is discrimination like a fence that keeps out new ideas. New information cannot enter, and old beliefs cannot get out. Please consider the fact that a person may not even recognize he's doing it."

"In the Biblical times, there are stories of villages protecting itself by building high walls around it, calling it a *fortress* or *stronghold* to withstand attacks. Their goal was to protect the people's center of living, like opinions, and attitudes. The fortified structure kept out invaders, but unknowingly kept the people from seeking life outside. Some may think of a stronghold as a beautiful thing, but after further analysis, their haven could be their paradox. Analyzing their approach, the true stronghold is in their minds. What is incredible to me is that in this age of advancement, people continue to live in their personalized stronghold. There is a synonymous term I use called tradition."

"Tradition is often spoken with pride. However, consider this caveat. Traditional thinking can lock minds on how things were and are. Creative thinking and advancement are lost in tradition. The saying that leopards cannot change their spots is true, but people can. This is good news, but this person must act to see change."

Dr. J.'s introduction provoked me to reflect on myself? Have I practiced discrimination toward others? This was the first time that I have been challenged with this. My mind drifted to a past event. There comes a time in life when every person takes their wilderness journey. I hark back to a sermon about a biblical character named Moses. He was called to lead the Israelites out of Egypt from the Pharaoh's bondage. The story told that God prepared Moses to free the slaves and were directed to live in a region that was called their *Promise Land*. Although the Israelites were physically freed, they never freed their mind. Their slave mentality blocked them from having hope of making it to their Promise Land. They became master complainers. Then complained about having to leave Egypt. They complained about having to travel. They complained about not getting to their destination fast enough. They complained about those who complained. No, just kidding there.

It was amazing to me how the first generation of Israelites never made it to their Promise Land, and in return for their horrible disposition, they spent forty years walking in the wilderness of the lost. How would I have felt having to walk in circles for forty years because of someone else's negative attitude? Truly, it had to suck. Their mindset was their demise. The critic is a complainer whose motive is to negate the actions of those listening. My takeaway was that opportunities arise from a loss.

Every person experiences a wilderness period in their life. During this time, they may feel alone and frightened, but if they stay faithful to their goal, the journey will be victorious. I think the unknown can scare people, but this can be eliminated by action which can fuel your desire to aspire.

Precaution is advised to the frame of mind to the person with an unachieved goal. Accepting failing is okay but never subscribe to being a failure. Failure becomes repetitive to the person who accepts it. Every person has gifts and talents that are useful for the advancement of society.

My parents taught me to be content with life, but not comfortable. Comfort can be debilitating. A friend of mine shared a story about being comfortable with not owning a car. The truth was that he could afford the car but not the insurance, and we know it is illegal to drive without insurance. Since he lived on the metro bus line, he decided to ride public transportation. He was conscientious about saving his money, so he decided to buy a monthly bus pass. During this time, fanny packs were trending. A male fanny pack was great for carrying personal belongings. One day while waiting at the bus stop, he noticed that his current fanny pack wasn't large enough to hold his important items. After thinking about it, he came up with a solution. He went to an establishment where the bags were sold. He figured that he would purchase a larger, better-quality bag to fix the issue. While standing in the store, he heard his conscience talk to him. "Why are you willing to buy a larger fanny pack? Don't you understand that you are accepting your fate of not having enough money for a car and the insurance to cover it? Are you willing to accept mediocrity? Are you willing to accept this bus as your car?" He realized then purchasing a larger bag confirmed his belief that riding the bus was the best he could achieve. The more thought he invested in the idea of the fanny pack the more it blocked his creative thinking. It was that moment; he realized what he contemplated most would manifest in his life. He set down the bag and walked out. Shortly, things changed. He earned enough money to buy the car and the insurance. Changing his belief, changed his life. He understood being comfortable does not inspire increase.

I snapped back to the present to hear Juice saying, "One of the results of discrimination within a person's mind is the destruction of his psyche. This is where a stronghold can block out the good things coming from others. It can create callous behavior toward people who are challenged by their beliefs. If you haven't given much thought about forgiveness, know that it is a powerful tool that cheats the world. The act of discrimination communicates that a person has the authority to treat someone differently from others. I wonder if people understand that forgiveness isn't beneficial to the person who's being held accountable. No, it is beneficial to the person holding the grudge. It frees the forgiver from consuming energy. I think about how this disease impacts the children."

Our guest speaker, Sandra Chisolm, will lead the group

exercises. She is a behavioral psychologist who owns a private practice. The internet is great! I quickly researched her background which is impressive. She appears to be candid, humorous, and a classy dresser. I love her shoes. Her sense of humor is great to hear.

On a sheet of paper, Ms. Chisolm asks everyone to describe an experience of when they've experienced discrimination. If they felt they've never experienced, they were to indicate that. Afterward, the staff would fold the paper in half to be placed in a basket located at the center of the table. The group would later revisit their answers during the second half of the workshop. She continued, "Blame is used often as a coping skill, or a scapegoat, when things aren't favorable. Let us look at the interaction between parent and teacher of a student failing school. The parent may be quick to place blame on the teacher and the teacher may reciprocate by blaming the parent for the child's poor performance. It can be an unlikeable roller-coaster ride."

"My research is initiated on the thinking processes of people. Thinking sounds simple, right? I think so but we are in an age when people are constructively processing. Did you know your thought influence comes from those you live with and many outside influences from institutions we think are not harmful? Sometimes the influence is so subtle that you don't know you're influenced. Understand that a person can receive stimuluses from society, parents, friends, and even movies or music videos. My goal is to assignment to survey us. I want us to take the time to reflect on our beliefs and why we do so. Also, I want to know who, in the group, can accept the idea of challenging their beliefs. I want to see who will move forward in making their life better for the good of society."

"The current state of our declining educational system is adequately funded. I believe certain groups of legislators aren't looking to change this antiquated system. More money is made from a broken system than a well-run system. Albeit not all school districts experience low performing results. This crude behavior of our students is a cry of help. They want the adults to take their authority and run things. Your challenge is simple yet complex. Blaming is irresponsible, unacceptable, and unproductive. It does not help the advancement of our children. First, I thought we needed to inspect the discriminatory issue between teachers and the students. Consider the fact of what will happen if we leave this monster unchecked? To heal this disease, it's going to take brave souls."

"I want you to have a sound view of bravery. It is not having the absence of fear but having the courage to act even in a state of fear. Fear paralyzes and discrimination is a form of fear. It is a weapon to deny people's rights. To understand others, a person should be open to know others. It is like polluted stagnated water. To understand this statement is to think of a river. A river has a constant flow that feeds many forms of life."

Listening to Chisolm, I thought about a cure for discrimination. I know for some it is difficult to change but with resolve it can be done. Decision, desire, and belief are the qualities my parents instilled in me. Contrary to what people may believe, the action of good is more powerful than the action of evil. As educators, we are here to implement growth. Nurturing is useful, but to really support our kids they need more action than our talk.

I tuned back into Chisolm ending her thought. Dr. J. took the lead. He divided the staff into groups of four. Each group was provided with a written scenario. It was designed to test each person's belief system. Each was required to write a response about how they would react to their given scenario. Afterwards, they would compare theirs with the others in the group. We had a time limit of thirty minutes. Each member was assigned a number, which was placed in what we called the response basket. Each member was assigned a role. Instead of calling out a person's name, a number was assigned but the cool part to this feature was that no other persons in the group knew each other's number selection. I thought this approach was clever. I like this inquiry process which allows a peek into a person's thinking while keeping their identity confidential. Sandra coined this workshop as The Critical Friends Group (CFG). The participants are permitted to ask questions to gain a better understanding, but the person asked was not permitted to respond with an answer. Sandra shared that our purpose was not to defend but provoke perspective.

When the thirty minutes were completed, the buzzer sounded. During the process, I heard engaged interaction from a group within my proximity. Their dialogue was meaty with provocative questions being asked. Effective communication is fundamental. The groups were asked to rotate to different stations. Mrs. Chisolm called different numbers of the members to share aloud their perspective of what was asked. I thought about what impact on us this would have. The questions are what stimulates intellectual growth.

Mrs. Chisolm guided us through three challenging and rewarding sessions. At the end of the workshop, I personally felt challenged and renewed. I felt as though I wanted to accomplish more at work. It was like having my sinuses clear to breathe easier. This influence of discrimination can seep in from various channels, especially family. A family, in its loving form, can easily transfer this disease. Kids won't know they are infected until they socially mix together.

Modeling is a powerful teaching tool. Some teachers instruct how they were taught. Should their style be questioned or their effectiveness? The answer is subjective and something to ponder, which brings up this issue. Are teachers amenable to altering their teaching style to meet the needs of their students? There is not one best practice to do anything. How else will we find new ways to do things if we keep a closed mind? The members of this group were asked to question themselves. How do we become better at our craft? Chisolm posed two questions for us to walk away with. First, why are we doing what we are doing? Second, is what we are doing the best action?

An idea came to me that I needed to share with Dr. J. I have this idea that our teachers should attend a sales seminar. I thought about the field trip Juice, and I attended. It was enriching for me to see other models in action. My intellectual eyes opened to see that an organization's success is understanding its people. This makes sense because educators are in the people business. Productive sales happen when the customer feels a connection with the salesperson. For our educators to excel, they need to be a people's person. In a chaotic environment, it is easy for teachers to not like students and the students to not like their teachers. Truth be told, the greatest gains come through invested relationships. A gardener cannot make the plant grow, but he can provide the optimum conditions for maximum growth. Likewise, a teacher cannot make a student learn but they can provide the optimum environment for growth. When students feel safe in their environment, a healthy exchange happens.

It is the school's obligation to provide a rich culture that fosters academic and social growth, and by rich, I mean to edify our students to creatively think, and problem solve. They need a safe school zone where they have the freedom to learn, create, challenge, and aspire. The adults are the caretakers and protectors to make that happen.

My sea of undulated thoughts floated toward the description of a superhero. This superhero moves separately from the crowd because of his truth. Privacy is paramount. Consider the famous. Most of them do not have any privacy when they go out in public. Superheroes face the same. They lack a private life. Once the public knows of the superhero's lair, it would be impossible to enter or leave their peaceful space without the paparazzi camping there. Fame comes with a price, and with a responsibility that most would have difficulty handling. Then I think of Dr. Juice Jordan. How does he manage his fame? I think back to a previous conversation with him. I reflected on his comment when he accepted the fact, he could not save everybody, nor did he try, even though he never stopped expecting a person's best. Facing that fact released his burden of trying to do something one person cannot do. Truth is, a person can only do as much as he thinks he can do, and the more he believes, the more he does. Everyone is responsible for himself.

I smile at myself. I can be so philosophical at times. Being an only child forced me to be in the company of my parents. Listening to their conversation formed my mature personality. In the spectrum of life, people can deny themselves their right to achieve their positive goals. I know teachers who went above and beyond to help a student, and despite their efforts, those students resisted their help. There are people around us that do not want other's help and some do not want to be saved from their own destruction. Whether we like it or not, they have the right to underachieve, be mediocre, or be at the top of the bottom in life. I have witnessed Jordan fighting for the handworkers. There is always opposition, but you do not have to succumb to defeat. Jordan believes he is unconquerable, and now I believe that I am also. He doesn't set his sight on the obstacle, but the vision. Juice thanks the world for its resistance. If it were not for failing schools, what would be his purpose? This challenge is his reward. I reckon as the medical doctor needs the physically sick, Dr. J. needs the educationally ill.

My dad told me a story about when he and mom bought their first house. The front yard was beautifully laid with Bermuda sod, but the backyard was bare but seeded. Over time the seeds only produced sparse grass, and mostly unsightly weeds. It was truly unattractive. He was saddened about it until a friend educated him on how to fix the issue. He told my dad that although it looked unattractive now, it was temporary. The weeds presently had a purpose. They're there to prevent the soil from eroding which allows the little grass there to root without washing away. He encouraged my dad to continuously plant more grass seeds. Eventually, this process would allow new growth to overtake the weeds. I made a connection with this analogy to our students. I know that some of us do not like to accept it, but the undesirable has purpose. We may not always see the why or agree with it, but it is there. Throughout the process, the magnanimous individual helping must keep faith and keep moving.

This workshop has done more than I had expected. It created a new perspective within me, causing me to genuinely introspect my values. I have become open to the idea of questioning myself. I want to challenge myself with doing the right thing before I act. I only hoped the staff absorbed this information with a new intense fire as I did. It is wrong for a teacher to deny a student an opportunity to succeed because of not liking the student. How would they feel if an administrator would deny them an opportunity for advancement because of being liked? Trading someone else's shoes is a good practice to adopt when making decisions.

I increased my dimension of thought. The world can be such a wonderful place if people release their fears. I believe that people would like to believe that if they keep their thoughts to themselves, no one will know their true thoughts. However, I beg to differ. I believe in what we feel the universe brings about, whether we speak it or not. It is just a matter of time before those feelings are manifested. Our thoughts form our actions, and our actions impact those around us. Can educators be completely objective with their students? I do not know. Should teachers be completely transparent with their students? Honestly, in this age the hurdle is too high. I guess anything is possible, but probable? The politically correct answer is easy to give but it poses a problem.

I looked at my watch. Finally, it was time for the workshop to end. Juice thanked everyone for attending and wished all a relaxing weekend before returning to work. We had two days remaining with the students, followed by post planning and then we could call it quits to a productive school year. I am sure the teachers will enjoy their well-deserved summer break. I know I will; even though I needed to report for the summer it did not bother me. We would have banker's hours, and not having the teachers and students around makes a huge difference while we wrap up and prepare for the upcoming year. Two months for a summer break sounded like a long time, but the new school year comes fast. I had much to prepare for. These months were like the offseason for an athlete. Champions prepare for their upcoming season in the off-season. I adopted this approach. My craft is who I am, and I know to be the best at something meant that I needed to be at the top of my game.

I enjoy the times when I reflect on my life's journey and victories, failures, and the relationships I've made. Are others like me when they catch themselves smiling about things? Thought is powerful. It shapes our life and impacts those nearby. My wish is that more people would be self-aware of this fact to activate the champion within. Our society wants everything immediately, but a journey is to be savored, not rushed. I like to take my time when I eat a slice of moist, decadent Butter Cream Vanilla Cake. I savor each bite from the icing to the buttery bottom of the cake. When I am sitting there, I reminisce on the good times in my life. It is a moment that I wished never would end, but it does. No matter, I made sure I enjoy that journey. What good is it to take a trip just to see how fast you can get through it? The pleasure is in the present time. This present is a gift that must be appreciated.

The final days for the students have passed and post planning is history. The days are beautifully mild and sunny. It seems like the opposite was the rule when it came to our climatic conditions. The winter temperatures were mild, and the summer temperatures are cool. I am not complaining. I enjoy it. The temperatures hover around eighty degrees. It is perfect convertible weather. I wished I could own one, but for now my sunroof works just fine. I love the sun beaming down on me with a gentle rush of cool breeze every so often while driving. The sunroof adds an airy feel to the interior of the car.

Today, Dr. J. arranged a catered lunch for the summer staff. The food is coming from one of my favorite restaurants called Season's Bistro. I have dined before at this well-respected establishment and love their cuisine. I figured it was something important that he wanted us to accomplish. Outside of related work issues, Juice kept his matters clandestine.

The morning passed quickly. My expectation of what we were having for lunch stayed on my mind. I was agreeable with the menu. I finished my last task in my office and made my way to the conference room. As I traveled through the main office, this wonderful aroma grabbed my nose. I saw Dr. J. sitting with a casual posture at the conference room table. I took the seat directly across from him. We chewed the fat while waiting. The conversation was enjoyable as he shared some life moments and talked about the vision for the upcoming school year and the new staff coming aboard. He took a moment to praise my growth as a leader. His compliment resonated in me. It is a beautiful thing when someone you respect gives genuine praise. He shared how he was impressed with my commitment to my job and my growth in my decision-making. To hear him compliment me meant the world. I smiled when he said it but in truth, I felt as though I wanted to cry. He shared his sentiments for Season's food. Juice agreed to several dessert options. Excitement washed over me when I saw one of my favorites. It was the delectable Death by Chocolate Cake. Juice decided he would have a slice of Banana Pudding Cheesecake.

It was at this moment he shared the news of his retirement. I was flabbergasted. His news made me feel like I was blindsided in a car wreck. Indubitably, he chatted up his love of being in the trenches with us all, but he felt it was his time to let it go. The emotional enjoyment of my dessert was muffled after hearing his announcement. Many thoughts filled my mind as I had trouble wrapping my head around this. Am I being selfish to feel like this? How could he walk away from doing so much good for our future leaders? In shock I was. By the nature of this lunch, I should have anticipated he wanted to tell us something, but I never thought it would be this. My stare was blank, and my jaw dropped. "Ms. Knight, be careful. You wouldn't want anything to fly in," he said with a smile. It took me a second before I caught on to what he meant.

After thinking about his news, I took a respite from eating my dessert. A potpourri of sadness, anger, and happiness filled my head. There are not many like him in this profession that I know. Eventually, my mind thought forward about his replacement. It would have to be somebody special, confident in their abilities and committed to the leadership development of the group. My desire to know urged me to ask, "Dr. J., do you know who your replacement will be?" "Yes," he answered as he continued, "I love watching Marvel and the Detective Comic movies. There is a little kid inside me when I watch them. I get lost in the characterization of the protagonist and antagonist. I know this may sound unexpected, but I push for a strong, dark villain. In the end, I want to see a victorious superhero. The storyline is so much better when the villain is portrayed as undefeatable. I think the villain helps develop the superhero. The superhero's character and strength are tested and that is when he must tap into his potential. Something else for an individual to consider is that an enemy is often considered to be external but what about the enemy of fear. To overcome this *in a me* calls for action. This is when his true power rises."

"A superhero is selfless and fights for justice. He fights for an idea greater than himself, and it is that idea that inspires others to join. If the justice, he fights for is his personal gain he simply becomes a vigilante fighting for his own cause. The fight only lives as long as he lives. Through his demise, the meaning and strength behind his actions is eliminated. However, fighting for an idea cannot be killed. It makes him powerful and inspirational. A superhero knows that the idea of truth and freedom must live through those who believe. Ms. Knight, that is why I selected you to be on my team. I believed that you could lead teachers in this vision of teaching students to become better thinkers."

"Now, to the answer of the next principal. It will be someone who I know and trust. I have had an opportunity to work with this person before and I feel confident about their abilities. I am sure you will approve as well. There is no doubt in my mind the staff will be in great hands. May I request one thing from you? Please do not ever settle for mediocrity. Trust yourself and the decisions you make for this team. This team needs your leadership."

"So, Juice, who is it?" impatiently asking. He smiled, "Knight, you aren't annoyed, are you?" Smiling partially, I knew then I needed to calm myself. "The new principal is you." Shocked, speechless, and happy was this moment for me. I was happy but caught off guard. I did not see this coming nor envisioned that I was ready. Dr. J, continued, "Intuitively, I knew you were the one when we first met. I have had many protégés under my tutelage, but after meeting you, I sensed something special. I felt when you learned to do what I was doing and maximize yourself doing it, you would do even greater things than me. As an African American woman, you have the potential to leave a great legacy. Believe in your purpose, that you can, and you will, and you will be unstoppable. Take what you have learned and apply it. I will be around if you need me."

"During this last year together, you must increase your vision. Even though you are in the assistant principal's position, I want you to take the helm and become the public face of the school. I will not officially announce my retirement until the last day of the next school year. I do not want any unnecessary distractions for our teachers and students. I am not looking for any fanfare. The sign of a great leader is one who understands how to walk away leaving an effective system intact." The only reaction I could muster was to shake my head in agreement. I stated, "Juice you know I'm committed, and I shall do what is required." My thoughts swirled in my head. I reminisced on Jordan's wisdom shared over the years. Success in any organization is built on having the right people doing the right thing in the right system. Did I catch every word spoken? I did not know. I think the residual of the shock from his news lingered. We finished lunch and continued with our work. It was later that afternoon when I noticed a higher level of confidence in my actions. Throughout that day, the reminder of his leadership praise was conscious.

Something to think about: Questions can force the sender beyond their opinion. They can cause the person to think about the what and the where of the intent of the conversation. Taking time to analyze the issue and moment helps the person asking to frame the question objectively.

As a leader, are you in the mode of telling others what you want or need to be done or do you practice asking?

_____

_____

_____

_____

_____

_____

_____

_____

_____

_____

_____

_____

_____

_____

_____

_____

_____

How can asking improve the working relationships?

_____

_____

_____

_____

_____

_____

_____

_____

_____

_____

_____

_____

_____

_____

_____

_____

_____

_____

_____

As a leader, do you provide time at the end of the meeting for decoding and analyzation? What is the importance of building your meetings around questions with your staff or the group?

_____

_____

_____

_____

_____

_____

_____

_____

_____

_____

_____

_____

_____

_____

_____

_____

_____

_____

_____

9

"A hero can be anyone, even a man doing something as simple and reassuring as putting a coat around a little boy's shoulder to let him know that the world around him had not ended."

--Batman, The Dark Knight Rises.

I concluded my day with reflection on the retirement news from Juice. I took in his belief that I could be a revolutionary leader in this industry. He believes that a great leader isn't determined by your gender or age. It is amazing that he saw it in me. When I decided on administration, my desire for promotion was to escape my classroom unhappiness. Even though my goal materialized, I never thought about the higher echelon. I was at a stage that my mind could not conceive becoming a principal, especially in such a short time. This experience has shown me that good things do come to those who do good. In this world, sometimes it appears the unjust are the victors, and if the just is not careful, they can fall into a trap of believing that perfidy pays. The Olympic torch has been passed on to me and I accept carrying it.

A surge of power, a sense of belief fills me when I think like this. Hey, why stop at being a principal? One of our past conversations surfaced in my consciousness. I did not get it then but now I do. Juice shared his reasons for hiring me were my qualities of righteousness, commitment, and people skills. I wanted to believe in the good nature of the people at my former school, but over time it didn't matter how much I wanted to believe, it wasn't going to change the people. I suppose there is no hope without despair. Most importantly, Dr. J. complimented on my teachable nature. I value what he has to say. He believes in people, the right people. His words ring clear in my mind, "Right people focus on the right things while wrong people destroy productive environments. Influential leaders encourage their people to act on what's right. Turning things around always starts the leader. The body has no choice but to follow the lead of the head. If a body is diseased, first diagnose the head. Typically, faulty thinking is the underline cause. Teachers and students are waiting for leaders to implement this concept. Just as superheroes guard and protect humanity great leaders fight for their team. Educational morality must be restored. The world is waiting for brave people with moral character. These words must be spoken with hope that they will fall onto listening ears, and may the figurative deaf awaken soon? Ms. Knight, you may experience some apprehension within after reflecting on this conversation, but you will adjust. In the beginning, you will take your lumps while fighting for goodwill, but your ego will heal quickly. You will accept that your efforts are for something bigger than you. Do not consume energy battling enemies. A golfer knows there are sand traps; he sees them but knows to avoid them. His focus is his target, not the distractions. Be aware that your actions will reveal enemies and allies. During this work, I must inform you that you will experience loneliness. You will be misunderstood and there will be days when you may second guess your purpose of what you are doing. However, take time to meditate on your mission and you will find clarity. When you do get what I am saying, I mean feel comfortable, you will be propelled to incredible heights. That is living life to the fullest."

*Five years forward...*I think about Juice. My memory of him is etched in my mind. I make my daily rounds throughout the school. Dr. Dexter Moore is my assistant principal. I recruited him after taking the reins from Juice Jordan. Dr. Moore is a strong, effective administrator. I saw that quality in him like Dr. J. saw in me. Moore is from Wichita, Ks. Before his interview, I took the initiative to call Mr. Guice, his former principal, regarding his background. He confirmed Dexter to be a strong administrator. In Guice's opinion, Dexter's classes were so disciplined that he granted him the authority to handle the discipline in the school. This is a great compliment and trust. Most principals put on a false impression that their school cannot run without him or her. I asked Mr. Guice if Dr. Moore was such a great asset, what was his motivation for leaving? Apparently, Dexter's decision to move to a different setting was influenced by the geographical location he wanted to raise his son. Moore has the right tools to be great in this business. He is what I call an administrator of the future. He loves educating, disciplining, and being around children, which are important qualities. I like how he interacts with the students. He spends much of his time out of his office with the students during classroom transitions. He invests time with the boys and girls who like basketball. They often play during their lunch period or after school. When the time comes, I have no qualms endorsing him for a principal's position. He is fresh out of the classroom, so I felt it would be easier for him to adjust to our system.

I transitioned my thoughts back to Juice. Now, as a principal, I relish the challenges that come my way. The cogs in our gears at Bethune Middle are turning smoothly. Teacher absence is minimal. To me this indicates they enjoy this environment. I see happiness in their smiles. The hallways are pleasant during transition. Our students genuinely greet the teachers with reciprocation. I hear a loud voice, "Ms. Knight, tell Darrius he's doing too much." It is Jasmine with her hand up in the air, pointing at Darrius. I smile. I understand now that kids like you when they say the craziest things to you. What can I say? They are kids. That is what they do. I have my moments when I think some are brain damaged. Often, they are impetuous and do not think about issues critically. I think I am on to a book titled *Brain Damaged*. Anyway, I knew it was an affectionate moment for Jasmine. I respond, "Jazzy!" Calling her by her nickname energized her. Kids love it when you give them a nickname.

I make my way back to my office. There is a letter on my desk. Intrigued, I open it and read the opening lines. *Dear Ms. Knight, I am sad to write that Dr. Juice Jordan expired yesterday morning. His body will be available for viewing next Saturday afternoon at 1:00 PM.* Nooo, it cannot be! Juice Jordan gone? Frozen in disbelief, I am unable to move. Minutes passed before I could sit down to recoup before I could think about leaving my office. This man was dear to me. He believed in me, and I am eternally grateful. I reminisce on our moments together, sharing professional and life experiences. I sat for a few minutes which seemed more like thirty minutes. Time at this moment seemed warped. Slowly, I could feel the life return in my legs. In our busyness, we overlook mortality. I think we blindly live life as though death is not a part of life. It is not a subject we consider until someone experiences it. There is a realization we each must face regarding this fact. We should not be afraid, instead we should celebrate our contributions. For me, this is my moment of awareness of why I should live each day with vigor, as though it was my last. I collected myself. As I pass my mirror, I gave self that last check before leaving the office. Things were in order. I attempt to dissipate the fog of sadness with a smile before entering the hallway.

Lethargically I make it through the day. I did not care to stick around the office. I went home. As I entered my driveway, it dawned on me that I really don't remember much of what happened at work today. This is a scary thought. I let myself into the house and immediately went to the kitchen for a glass of Mango Cranberry juice. Casually, I make it to my chaise. It is so comfortable that I often fall asleep on it. I sat and reflected on my memories of Juice Jordan.

I remembered that I didn't check the mail. I don my flip flops and walk to the mailbox. I remove the mail and notice a letter addressed from Juice Jordan. Immediately, I open the letter to read it. My eyes welled with tears as I reminisced on some favorite moments together. I laugh to myself. Without noticing, I walk toward my garden in the backyard. Somehow the letter and the atmosphere of the garden went together. I suppose there was peace in both. I hear the singing of the birds. The butterflies fly close to me but make sure not to touch me. It was like they wanted me to see them frolicking. I make my way to sit on my swing. I smell the sweetness of aroma emanating from the flowers. Further in the letter, Juice shared intimate feelings of how he felt when he learned of his illness. *I am sick and scared. I am in a territory where I am unsure how to navigate. For most of my life I have felt in control, but now I feel vulnerable. I have heard that being alone hurts, but I realize that it is loneliness that hurts. I wanted to tell someone, but I knew that telling people that you are sick brings pity. Human nature causes people to gossip and spread unnecessary information. I did not want that. Even if that was not the case, I did not want that thought weighing on my mind. The closer I progressed; certainty reassured me. Completing my mission satisfied me regardless of my health. I wanted you to know that I left satisfied and content. Keep hold of your purpose.*

I did not know. Sympathy filled me. Sometimes, people mean well, but they inappropriately do the wrong thing which adds to the damage. Knowing Juice, even if I had been aware of his condition, he would not have allowed himself to be a distraction. Jordan was a man of focused achievement, and nothing could impede that.

His concluding statement eloquently closed out his letter. It is what I call a New York Theatre play of life. *My time at bat came and went. I gave my best to the world, and I hit a grand slam homerun. In the end, some people will say they wished they had done more with their time on earth, but not me. I gave it my all with no leftovers to be stored. My gift was helping young people to become better thinkers for the advancement of the world. When I met you, I knew my ending was near. It was time for my decrease and your increase. I knew I did not have the luxury to bring you to speed with taking baby steps. Fortunately, I saw by your ability that once you grabbed a hold of the purpose you were undeniable. I listened to you and how you felt about your students. You are a game changer. Your reception of this letter means that I have passed. Please do not mourn my demise but continue to do the work you have started and continue to inspire others to be champions. After my retirement, I continued to keep you in my sights. I needed to see for myself that you would manifest my prediction. Your growth and impact took off faster than I thought. Be an eagle, always be unstoppable.* In my mind, I answer, "I am. Thank you."

I recalled my first year succeeding Juice as principal. It was the first day of school that I noticed a letter on my desk addressed by him. I had only time enough to read the first line before going to my duty post. The students were about to be released from the café to their first period. I opened it and read the title *Standards Matter*. I smiled and walked to my post.

Do you hold your colleagues accountable at work? How?

How do you hold yourself accountable?

Takeaway:

If you want people to think, you must get them to exercise their brain, not merely follow orders.

If you are in a supervisory position, how do you approach your colleagues, managing or coaching? What does that look like to you?

_____

_____

_____

_____

_____

_____

_____

_____

_____

_____

_____

_____

_____

_____

_____

_____

_____

_____

_____

_____

In evaluating your current job, are you being stimulated and challenged? How can you challenge and stimulate others through questions?

_____

_____

_____

_____

_____

_____

_____

_____

_____

_____

_____

_____

_____

_____

_____

_____

_____